Dandelion Wishes

Leteisha Anne

DEDICATION

While I believe that anyone can make things happen for themselves and create the life they desire, I understand that no one does it alone, myself included.

Without my grandmothers, Margaret and Louise, this book would not have happened. Early on, they encouraged me and helped in ways I can't begin to count.

This book, and all that it stands for, is dedicated to them.

ACKNOWLEDGMENTS

If there is anyone to thank for helping me along this journey, it would be my talented and kind hearted editor, Tracy. Without her, there is no way this book would be finished and sitting in your hands.

I would also like to thank my Mom, Darlene, my sisters, Payton and Rickelle, as well as my fiancé, Kevin for the love and support they have given me along this journey.

Chapter One

At eight years old you don't really understand much about life, or anything for that matter. All you worry about is playing with your friends, loving your pet, dressing up in your mom's best clothes when she isn't looking, and learning how to apply that pretty, red lipstick you found while you were at your grandmother's house. You don't normally fret about the future, or where you are going to end up when you hit your thirties or forties. That's just too far away. Heck, it's going to take forever before you're old enough to drive, let alone have a career and actual life of your own. So, instead of worrying about what's to come, you just focus on the now; you focus on what's happening right this second in front of you. Well, I did too. That is, until the day my aunt died.

I was just eight years old when my mother got the call. My Aunt Lisa was driving home from work when a drunk driver swerved into her lane and hit her head on. We were told she died instantly and didn't suffer. Thank goodness. It would have been easier, I think, if she were older, but Aunt Lisa was only forty-two and had so much to live for. She didn't have any kids due to cancer in her early twenties, ruining any chance she had in ever conceiving, but she did have a beautiful home, a loving boyfriend and a job many girls dream of: she was a model and actress, and she had just finished filming her last movie when the accident occurred.

Naturally, everyone who knew her well took it pretty hard. She was my mom's only sibling, her older sister, so needless to say, she had the toughest time with the entire situation. Growing up, they did everything together. My mom and Aunt Lisa went to school together, attended community functions and parties together, they even went to the same university when they were old enough. My

1

mom was by her side through every chemo treatment and hospital stay and when my mother got married, Aunt Lisa helped plan the entire thing. When I and my sister were born, she was the first one to meet us at the hospital no matter how busy her schedule was. Aunt Lisa just had that special something about her that had you fall in love with her the second you met her.

So, when she passed, my mom hit the ground at a devastating speed. She developed a form of depression that not only had an effect on her, but had an effect on everyone she lived with. She and my dad would argue more often, the house became a disorganised mess and she would break down crying at any little thing. She had become very reserved and quiet, even though she was getting weekly counselling, but even after all of that, she made sure to hold me and my sister Demi extra tight every single night as she tucked us in to bed.

Months passed after the funeral and nothing new or exciting ever happened. My sister, Demi, and I, however made sure to stay as close as ever. We have only a two-year age difference so it was as though she was one of my best friends. We would colour, play teacher, and attempt to braid each other's hair almost every day. Luckily for me, my two other best friends, Miranda and Amber, loved my sister, so we played together on a regular basis.

Despite the fact that Miranda and Amber were in and out of our house as much as we were during those years, it was several weeks after Aunt Lisa's passing that we again began what had been nearly weekly sleep overs and play-dates.

"I could ask Mom if you guys can come over after school on Friday and stay for the weekend," I suggested tentatively one lunch hour on the playground as we sat on the merry-go-round, aimlessly turning it with our feet. It felt weird, making plans to have fun, because everything had been so different in the last few weeks, but I missed the time we used to spend with our friends outside of school, and I knew that Demi did too. "Mom told us yesterday that there was a new box of things from Aunt Lisa. It came before…"

I paused. It was still difficult to talk about. Looking at the others, I could see that Miranda looked uncomfortable, Amber looked surprised and Demi…Demi had tears in her eyes, but looked at me almost hopefully.

"We can have a fashion show," I continued bravely, feeling just a bit stronger. "And maybe watch a movie before bed."

"There are always such nice things in the boxes from your aunt," Miranda said, glancing at Demi.

"I love the bracelets and necklaces," Amber sighed.

"I like the dresses," Demi kicked at the dirt. "Aunt Lisa was a movie star. I loved her dresses. I want to be a movie star when I'm big."

"I think that would be a lot of fun," Miranda chimed in. "If my mom says it's okay, I'll bring my new movie, *Frozen*. I haven't watched it yet, so this way we can all see it together. It looks really good. The girls on the front are pretty anyway."

"You *have* that? We were going to see it but Dad ended up working late and Mom had a cold that day," Amber paused briefly. "Do you think your bus driver will have cookies again Dixie? The monster cookies she had last time we came on your bus were really good."

Amber had a love for two things: Disney movies and dessert. The prettier the princess and the bigger the treat, the more she enjoyed both.

"I hope so," I replied. "It will be Friday and she usually has treats on Fridays. Last week she brought doughnuts and they were awesome."

"Yeah, mine had sprinkles on it and Dixie's had gooey stuff inside." Demi giggled.

The recess bell rang, indicating play time was over

and we scrambled up, heading for the school doors as a group.

"I'll ask Mom tonight," I said, but I was almost scared to hope that we could, just maybe, return to where we'd been before that phone call came.

That evening we asked our mother if the girls could come for a sleep over that weekend.

"Yay!" Demi shouted when Mom agreed to let the girls spend the night. "Yay-yay-yay! That means we get to watch Miranda's movie."

"What movie is that?" asked Mom.

"*Frozen*," I explained. "She said she might be able to bring it."

"As long as you girls clean up your messes this time and go to sleep when I tell you to. I don't want an episode like last time," Mom gave me *that* look.

Our last sleep over we had a bit of a mess in the spare room that we forgot to clean up. Clothes, colouring supplies, popcorn, Demi's dolls and their clothes had littered the floor, and on top of that, we stayed up two hours past our bed time telling stories and playing truth or dare.

"Yes, Mom," we both agreed.

"Is it alright if we have a fashion show with the clothes from Aunty Lisa? We promise to take good care of them and be extra careful," I asked quietly.

Mom paused for a second then turned to look us both in the eyes. You could tell she was hesitant and having flashbacks to when Aunty Lisa was still here.

"Let me tell you what," Mom sighed and bent down to our eye level. "If you promise to be careful with them and put them away nicely when you're done, then, yes you can have a fashion show upstairs and then quietly watch your movie in the spare room okay?"

"Okay, thank you, Mom," I gave her a hug and she squeezed back tightly before standing up again.

"You're welcome. Now get upstairs and get your homework finished. Supper will be ready in forty-five minutes. I will call the girls' moms and see if it's alright with them."

Demi and I both turned and made our way up the stairs to the spare room, which was also where we did all of our homework.

The next morning couldn't come soon enough.

"You can come. You can come!" Demi exclaimed to Miranda and Amber as we met them at the front doors to the school. "Did you get permission?"

"Yep, and I even brought my movie and Amber brought some new snacks. They sound really yummy," Miranda replied.

"Have you ever heard of jelly straws?" Amber asked. Both Demi and I shook our heads. "They're awesome! Mom bought me this tub over a month ago but I've been saving them for a special occasion. They're jello...in a straw, and all the colors taste different. The green ones are my favorite. They taste like apples."

After school was finished for the day, we headed for the school bus, all four of us climbing on and taking our seats. Miranda sat with me across from Demi and Amber.

"I think I saw a container of goodies." Amber whispered hopefully. "I wonder if they're for us. Ooh, I hope so. I hope they are monster cookies again. I love monster cookies."

Just then my bus driver, Mrs. Corbeil, stood up and announced that since it was Friday she did in fact, have a treat for everyone on the bus. As she walked down the aisle, each student was allowed to take one goody.

"I knew it!" exclaimed Amber with wide eyes and hungry lips as the bus driver made her way to our seat first; sitting in the front has its perks. "Thank you, Mrs. Corbeil, your monster cookies are my favorite thing in the whole wide world. They're even better than my mom's brownies, and she makes good brownies."

Mrs. Corbeil then chuckled, "Well, thank you, Amber, you are too kind. Would you girls like one as well?" She then let us each take one cookie each.

"Thank you," We all chimed together as she continued down the bus with her container.

Amber had her cookie gone within just a few bites when she leaned towards Miranda and I as we nibbled on ours. "I love your bus driver. I wish I had her *every* Friday." She then looked back towards Demi sitting by the window, who was examining which color of smarties were hidden throughout her treat. "Are you going to eat that? Because if you're not…"

"I'm going to eat it, so don't you even think about it. I just like to see what pretty colors are in it first." Demi then took a big bite out of her cookie and hid the rest from Amber.

Treats distributed, Mrs. Corbeil took her seat, started the bus and we were off.

It was a mere ten-minute drive from the school to our place so it was nice that we didn't have a long wait on the bus. Once we arrived in our yard and pulled to a stop, each of us grabbed our back packs and, one by one, left the bus.

"Thank you for the cookies again, and the ride," I thanked Mrs. Corbeil behind the others.

"You're welcome, my dear," she smiled at me. "Have a good weekend and don't get into too much mischief."

"We won't," I grinned back at her. I then headed towards the house with the others and the bus left our yard. Mrs. Corbeil and her Friday treats were a constant, and at that time, Demi and I needed that consistency in our lives.

Once inside, we tossed our bags on the floor by the door and went to the kitchen only to be greeted by my mother and grandmother, who were busy making pies for an upcoming farmers market. My mom didn't do much within the community anymore, but the farmers market was one thing that she and my grandmother had attended together every year for the past twenty years. I was glad she at least continued doing that. They were known in town for their delicious baking, especially their pecan pie. The recipe had been in the family for over one hundred years and they say it has a special ingredient that grandma's mom added to it years ago, but they wouldn't tell me what it was. I guess they thought Demi and I would tell someone and the word would get out and then no one would buy their pies because they could make it themselves. Either way, the pie tastes delicious and makes them a lot of money.

"Oh, well, look what the wind blew in," Grandma Marg called out. Her real name is Margaret, but Demi and I call her Grandma Marg. "Two of my most favorite grand-daughters and their two beautiful friends. Come give your grandma a hug."

Demi giggled and ran to give her a big hug.

"Grandma, you know we are your *only* grand-daughters, right?" I smiled and gave her a hug as well. Amber and Mirada giggled; they know how silly my family is.

"Well, of course I do. Why do you think you're both my favorites?" She winked at us. "Now, how was school? What did we learn today?" she asked as she bent down to Demi's height.

"I learned all about rainbows!" Demi stated excitedly. "Violet is my favorite part. Then Mrs. Kelly taught us how to read a clock. I like our alarm clocks upstairs better because they aren't hard to read at all."

"Well, good for you. It sounds like you had a very busy day, Demi. And how about you girls? What did you all learn?" Grandma asked us next as she straightened from Demi's level.

"Well, in math we worked on our multiplication and

in English we are going to start reading a new novel soon. So, we read a bit from it," Miranda mentioned.

"Yep, and in Science we started learning about different types of clouds," Amber added.

I told Grandma about our French class as well as Social Studies.

"Well, goodness me! It sounds like you all had a very busy day, and you know what? I have the perfect way to end a long school day."

Demi got excited. "What's that, Grandma?"

She then turned around and grabbed a tray of mini pecan tarts from the counter. Amber was almost drooling as we each took a tart.

"Thank you, Grandma," I said, taking mine.

"You're welcome, darlings."

Mom then piped up and asked if any of us had homework due on Monday. Happily, we had none, and were told to go either upstairs or outside to play so that she and Grandma could finish baking; we chose upstairs. After running up the stairs as fast as we could we all dove and jumped onto the spare room bed, the springs groaning under the onslaught.

"So, you all do realize what just happened there, right?" Amber asked once we all calmed down and got our giggles under control.

The rest of us sat up and just looked at her, confused.

"What?" I asked. "Realize what? That we made the bed slide when we jumped on it?"

Amber giggled. "Well, yeah, but no. We just got *two* treats today. First, a cookie, and then a tart *and* I still have my jelly straws! I wonder what's next? Hopefully popcorn tonight or chips, or more tarts…"

Miranda then shook her head. "Is that all you ever think about, Amber? Food?"

"Well, isn't that what everyone thinks of?"

We all giggled, shaking our heads. Miranda rolled her eyes.

"What?" Amber asked.

"Nothing, Amber," I said. "We got a new Candy Land game that used to be Mom's. Demi found it in the attic a few weeks ago. It's my new favorite game. Do you guys want to play?"

After we all agreed on playing Candy Land, and after a few minutes spent finding it in the closet, we set it up and taught Miranda and Amber how to play. It felt good and it felt normal. It felt like we were getting past the terrible things that had happened, and that life might just *be* normal again... soon.

Chapter Two

"Alright, so we have five cherry, five blueberry, twenty pecan, and five pumpkin pies. Twenty jars of jam, over one hundred pecan tarts, and twenty-four of all the other tarts. I guess we just have some bread and buns to make and we will be set to go. You have all the garden vegetables boxed and ready to go, yes?" Grandma Marg asked as she brought out the bread pans from the cupboard.

"Yes, the veggies are all ready," my mother replied, tidying away the mess and wiping down the counter.

"I'll set these in the back room until we are ready to leave tomorrow." Grandma then began carrying containers to the back room. "Doreen?" Grandma called out to my mother.

"Yes? What's wrong?" she asked, wiping her hands with a tea-towel.

"Oh, nothing's wrong, dear. I just found the box that was meant for the girls, tucked under the table. Were you planning on giving it to them soon?"

"Oh, yes. I told them about it the other day. I was going to give it to them this weekend. They wanted to have a fashion show with Miranda and Amber."

"I see, would you like me to give it to them? Or did you want to wait until after supper?"

"Um, you can give it to them now if you'd like. They can go through it and then come down for supper. I'll order pizza right away."

Grandma stared at my mother, where she could see the pain in her eyes, then, moving forward, she gave my mother a hug.

"It will be okay, dear. We all have each other. You are doing an amazing job. Don't ever forget that, okay?"

My mother teared up and quickly changed the subject as she wiped her cheek. "So, did you want all meat or pepperoni? You know what, I'll just get one of each and they can have left-overs for lunch tomorrow." She grabbed the phone off the counter and left to the living room.

As we were in the middle of playing Candy Land we heard a knock on the spare room door. Grandma peeked inside, "Hey, girls, I have a special surprise for you." All four of us looked up from the board game, excited.

"Are there any more tarts?" Amber asked, which then made my grandma giggle.

"No dear, no more tarts, but your mother is ordering pizza in for supper tonight, and I know how much you all enjoy a good slice of pizza." We all cheered for joy. "Also, I have here a special box that your mother asked me to give to you."

We calmed down and Demi and I looked at each other hopefully.

"Grandma? Is that Aunty Lisa's box?" Demi asked.

Grandma Marg smiled and told us that it was. "The only thing is that you have to be very careful not to damage anything in this box. Okay? Can you girls promise me that you will be extra gentle and put everything back in here when you are done?"

"Yes, Grandma. We'll put it in the closet when we're are done, too, so we don't forget where it is," I told her.

"Okay, good. Now, I will leave this with you and I'm going to finish helping your mom in the kitchen. We'll call you when the pizza arrives."

She put the box on the bed, gently closed the door, and went back downstairs to finish helping mom with the baking.

All four of us sat for a moment and stared at the box in silence before Demi and I looked at one another to decide who would open it.

"You can open it, Dixie," Demi finally said. "You're oldest."

I looked over at Demi sitting on the floor next to me. "Or we can open it together. This way it's even."

With that Demi smiled and shook her head. I grabbed the box from the bed and set it on the floor between us.

"You ready?" I asked.

"Yep," Demi replied. "One, two, three!"

On three, we both tore the box top wide open. When we looked inside all four of us gasped at the contents. The box was full of brightly coloured fabric and smaller boxes.

"Oh, my goodness!" Demi exclaimed as she picked a jewelry box out to examine. "Look how shiny this is! It must be made of real gold and diamonds. Look at the rubies, Dixie!"

I had to admit, that was a pretty nice box, but I wasn't interested in that. My entire focus was taken by the dark red, shiny material, and I knew it would be something special. Pulling it out, I realized how right I'd been; it was a long red gown. On Aunt Lisa, it would have swept the floor. On me, it would pool around my feet.

"This must be the dress Aunty wore to that awards night she went to last year," I held it up against my body, clearly far too big for my petite frame and size. "How does it look? Does it bring out my eyes?"

"Yeah, because you have red eyes, Dixie." Amber scoffed good naturedly. "You're so silly. That is a pretty dress though. You should try it on later when we have a fashion show."

Amber then reached into the box herself. "Oh, look at this blue one! It has jewels all over the neck part." She then held that one up too, and stood next to me. "Wow, it even has a slit up the side. This one would bring out your eyes better, Dix, because your eyes are blue, too. Not my green eyes, I wonder if there's a green dress in there?"

Demi and Miranda peered into the big box to check.

"Mm-nope. No green one, sorry, Amber, but there is a purple one, black one and... oh! Look at this white one and high heels and ooh, make-up!" Demi ruffled through the new findings and found a smaller box at the bottom, underneath everything.

"What's that?" Miranda asked her. Gently Demi brought the smaller box out so we all could see it. On top, held with a bit of tape, was a letter with our names written on it. With a confused look on her face, Demi handed me the box.

"You open this one, Dix."

My curiosity took over, and I grabbed the box, peeling the letter of the top. Slowly and carefully, not to rip the envelope or letter, I took it out and read aloud:

My dearest girls,

If you are reading this letter, it must mean that Dixie has graduated! I am likely away filming another movie or something crazy like traveling, so I wanted to have this ready for you in case I am not able to be there with you in person. So, congratulations my girl. I am so proud of you and how far you've come. It seems like yesterday that your parents brought you home in your pink blanket and hat. Where has the time gone? And Demi, my dear, only two more years and you will be graduating as well. I bet school is wonderful and you are acing everything. You both are so smart and talented. With that, I am giving you both a present to share. It's not money and it's not a trip, it's something so much better than that. Because you are both grown up and about to face the world, I wanted to give you something that will help you along this journey in life. In this box, you will find a series of books and a movie. These were the tools I had when I first got into acting and modeling. I'm not sure I would have made it without these. Actually, I likely would have given up and gone back to working at the bank in town. In these books and DVD, you will find the necessary tools to get you through life. It will teach you how to manage your thoughts and bring your greatest wishes and desires in life. This probably sounds a bit confusing right now, but once you read and watch this, everything will make perfect sense, trust me. I know what you two are capable of, and I know that whatever direction you choose in life, it will take you to the most incredible places. No matter what, always believe in yourself and always believe in each other. I cannot wait to see where you both end up. Bless your beautiful hearts. Give me a call when and if you ever need anything.

Forever loving,
Aunt Lisa

I then folded up the letter and looked at Demi who was still sitting on the floor, slightly confused.

"Well, clearly, we weren't supposed to get this smaller box until grade twelve is over." I said aloud. "Do you think we should open it? I mean, we aren't close to graduating. What do you think?"

After a moment of thought Demi decided that we should open it. "Well," she said, "She left it for us to open one day. I don't know why we couldn't now. I mean, let's do it and if it doesn't make sense we can tape it again and open it when we're older."

Demi and I stared at each other and then at Miranda and Amber who waited quietly for our decision to be made.

"Okay, let's open it," I said. We all sat back down into our little circle and pushed the bigger box out of the way as we placed the mystery box on the floor. I slowly picked the tape at the corner and pulled it away.

Once we were able to see what was inside, I suddenly began to feel excitement and confusion. Inside the box were books and a DVD called *The Secret*. I took the DVD out and handed it to Amber.

"Here, you hold this one," I then grabbed the books. The first one was called *The Secret* also, the second was called *Hero* and the last was *The Power*, all written by the same author, Rhonda Byrne. Once I showed the collection to Demi, she looked even more puzzled than I was. "The letter said that these are supposed to help us bring things into our lives…"

"How are books supposed to do that?" Miranda questioned. "Are they magic books?"

I look over the first book in my hand which was *The Secret*. "I don't think so," I said. "I think that they tell you *how* to get things. I'm not sure how that works though. Do you guys want to watch the movie and see what it's about? I think the books will be…"

Right then my mother called us for supper.

"Girls, pizza's here!" She called from the bottom of the stairs. "Wash up and get down here before it gets cold."

"Okay, be right down," I shouted back. "Well, what do you guys say? Do you want to eat and then watch the movie?"

"But what about *Frozen*?" Demi asked.

I thought about that for a moment before replying. "Okay, how about this. Why don't we watch *Frozen* tonight and then tomorrow we can all watch *The Secret*. Let's just have fun tonight and we will see what this one is about in the morning. Only, let's not tell anyone about this quite yet. Like, don't tell mom. We should watch it first and then maybe show her what we got. Then we can explain it to her better."

I don't know why it felt necessary to watch the movie that Aunt Lisa said would help before sharing it with our mother, but somehow, it did. Quietly, we washed our hands and headed downstairs, where Mom and Grandma waited with pizza.

"So girls, how was your game of Candy Land?" Grandma asked as we took our places around the table. "Your mother, aunt and I used to play that game all the time when they were little girls. My favorite is the princess."

"I like the princess, too, Grandma!" Demi exclaimed. "She's so pretty. But we didn't finish playing. You brought the box when we were just started."

"Oh, well, I'm sorry, dear. I should have let you finish."

"No, it's alright Grandma, we preferred the box anyway. Right, Dixie?"

"Right," I said. "She left us some really pretty dresses and shoes and jewelry and stuff." I peered around at the three other girls with a slight smirk before taking a bite of my pizza.

"Well, I'm glad to hear that. Now, what do you girls plan on doing after supper?" Grandma asked.

"I brought a movie for us all to watch. It's one we all wanted to see for a while now. It's called *Frozen*. It has real pretty princesses, a snowman that talks, a reindeer that's a pet and some handsome princes. But one prince is supposed to be mean." Miranda chattered away.

"That sounds like it's going to be a good one," my mother chimed in. "Would you girls like some popcorn and drinks to go with the movie? I can bring you some to snack on while you watch if you'd like."

"Thanks, Mom. Can we watch it in the theatre room? We promise to keep it extra clean and we will be extra quiet," I asked hopefully.

"Well, I don't know, maybe you should ask your father first," she then looked at my dad who was casually speaking to my grandmother at the far end of the table. Once breaking his conversation off, he replied with a 'yes'.

"As long as you girls help your mother with the dishes, tidy your rooms before bed and promise to be quiet. I have a lot of work I have to do in my office and can't have any distractions tonight. Do we have a deal?"

"Yes, Dad," I responded, excited for what was to come. The moment our dinner was finished, all four of us girls asked to leave the table and began clearing away the dishes.

After the kitchen and our bedrooms were in order, we all quickly put on our pajamas, grabbed some blankets and pillows, as well as a few much-needed stuffed animals and headed to Dad's new theatre room. Once inside, Miranda and Amber gasped. They had never seen an at home theatre before. The big projection screen on the far wall, the speakers all over the room, and the big theatre chairs taking up most of the floor space, had them both mesmerized.

"Well, what are you guys waiting for?" Demi demanded. "I want this chair!" she said as she took one of the inside chairs. "Dix, put the DVD on!" Demi wasn't allowed to touch the equipment, and knew that if she did, Dad would be angry.

I placed my blanket, pillow and stuffed dinosaur on my chair, grabbed the DVD from Miranda and carefully put it into the player. Once done, we all made ourselves comfortable and called mom to let her know that the movie was starting.

"Oh no!" Amber quickly stood up and began to race to the door.

"What is it?" Miranda asked as we all turned around to see where she was going.

"The jelly straws. I forgot the jelly straws! Don't start the movie without me. I will only be a minute. Not even, more like thirty seconds!" With that, she raced out the door, passed my mom and she was gone.

"What was that about?" My mother asked as she worked her way into the theatre room, hands full with a tray that consisted of two bowls of popcorn, four glasses of pop, a roll of paper towel and a bag of M&Ms. She then sat the tray down on the table, handed us each a glass of pop and began to pour the bag of M&Ms into the bowls of popcorn.

"Oh, she just forgot her jelly straws. She ran to get them," I told her.

"Yeah, she said not to start the movie without her," Demi added.

"I see," Mom replied. "Here." She handed us each a

glass and the popcorn. "Now, no spilling. But if you do, there's paper towels on the table. You girls have fun and keep quiet, Dad is busy, remember. Now your Grandma and I will be in the kitchen if you need us."

With that she left and Amber returned panting.

"Got 'em!" She exclaimed, climbing back into her chair. "*Now* we can watch the movie. Oh, popcorn! I love popcorn." Handing around handfuls of the straws, she grinned.

"Now, what do you do…" Miranda began to ask.

"So what you do with these babies is rip the top off with your teeth and slurp it back." Amber beamed.

"Here, I'll show you," Amber then ripped the top off her jelly straw and, sure enough, slurped it back as fast as lightning and giggled.

"I want to try," smiled Demi, ripping the top off and slurping back the contents of the straw, dribbling a bit and giggling.

"Me, too!" laughed Miranda.

Once the roar of laughter subsided and we all got comfortable, I started the movie.

Chapter Three

The next morning came quickly. Once we all awoke to the smell of bacon and eggs cooking, we made our way downstairs for breakfast. The house was quiet, but the sound of our mother stirring in the kitchen let us know it wasn't too early to be up.

"Well, good morning girls. How are we all this morning?" Mom asked cheerfully.

"We're good, Mom. We watched the whole movie last night before we fell asleep." I replied. "It was so good."

"Yeah, it's my new favorite movie," Amber exclaimed. "My favorite character is Elsa. She's so pretty and her hair is really nice. I want hair like her," she said as she ran her fingers through her own blonde curls.

Demi piped up next. "My favorite character is Olaf because he's *so* funny and I like snowmen. And I like warm hugs too! And I like when he says his nose looks like a little baby unicorn." She giggled and took her regular place at the table.

"And how about you two?" Mom asked Miranda and I as she finished making breakfast. "Who was your favorite character?"

After some thought, Miranda decided that Sven and Kristoff were both her favorites due to the fact that they always stick together. She says that Sven is cute and reminds her of her dog.

"I think my favorite is Anna. She's just so brave and always believes in Elsa. She knows she's not really a bad person like Hans. I don't like Hans at all. He's so mean." The others agreed with me easily; Things seem that simple when you are eight. "We weren't too noisy, were we Mom? We tried to be quiet."

Mom then placed a large plate of bacon and eggs on the table along with some orange juice and milk. "No, you girls weren't noisy at all. Your father was able to get all of his work and phone calls finished. Speaking of which, where is your father? He said he would be down to eat with you girls before he had to go out this morning. He is going to run to the office and then, when he gets back, your grandma and I are going to head to the farmers' market for the day, okay? I better go find him so he gets going soon. You girls start eating before your eggs get cold."

Mom left the room, and after a few moments of silence as we dished up our plates, Miranda asked us about the other movie.

"So, do you guys still want to watch it? I mean, *The Secret*? Or do you want to wait till you're older?"

Demi and I looked at one another curiously as we took a bite of our bacon.

"I think we should watch it," I said after a few seconds. "I mean, what could it hurt, right? Aunty Lisa said it's supposed to help us figure out our lives. Maybe it will show us something and it will make sense. Maybe it will tell us what we should be when we grow up. Should I be a writer? A teacher? An astronaut? I think it would be cool to see what it says. What do you think, Dem?"

"I want to watch it," Demi stated. "Maybe it will teach me how to me a model like Aunty. That way I will be able to wear pretty clothes and shiny jewelry just like her and be in magazines."

She then practiced her classic duck lips, complete with a side shoulder pose, making us laugh.

"Alright. After breakfast, we will watch it and see what it says."

Our parents then walked back into the kitchen together and we finished our breakfast with calm conversation.

"Mom, can we watch another movie in the theatre room? We will be quiet, I promise." I asked hopefully after the kitchen was cleaned up and organized.

"Another one?" she asked. "Well, I suppose, but

that's it with the movies and TV until tonight then. Once your movie is done, you girls go and play outside for the day. The sun is shining and it's supposed to be one of the last nice days for a while. They say it's going to rain for the next few days, off and on. So, go watch your movie, then get dressed and head outside. By the time it's over your dad should be back and I will be gone, so I will tell him what you will be doing. Just let him know when you go out, he will likely be in his office most of the day again. Come in when you are ready for lunch and he will warm up that left over pizza for you girls, alright?"

"Okay, Mom. Thank you." The others followed Demi to the theatre room while I ran upstairs to get the DVD. Within just a few moments I raced back. "Alright, I'll put it in." I said, out of breath.

"Holy Dix, how fast did you run?" Miranda asked. "You look like you just ran three laps in the gym."

"Yeah, your face is all red. You didn't have to run that fast. We were fine waiting for you," Amber commented as I placed the DVD into the projector and shut the lights off.

Demi whispered and looked around cautiously, "I wanted her to hurry," no one else heard her. We all snuggled in and got ready to watch a movie that would change our lives forever.

The movie ended and we all sat in silence for a few moments, looking around at one another. We weren't a hundred percent sure what to say.

"Well, what do you guys think?" I asked. "I mean, do you think that this stuff is for real? Does that mean we attract everything into our lives? They did use some pretty big words in there but I think I kinda understand it."

"I think I get it too, It's like when you wish on a shooting star or a wish bone," Amber explained. "You see a shooting star or you get the big half of a wish bone when you break it and make a wish and then you sit back and wait for your wish to come true."

Demi got excited for a moment, "Oh, like when I got the big half of our wish bone, Dix, and wished for my princess bed and then for my birthday I got it. I didn't tell anyone except my teddy bear that I wanted it. And I don't think my teddy told anyone. Wow, I think that stuff *is* for real."

"I agree," Miranda piped up. "I mean, they wouldn't make a movie like this for nothing, right? And your aunty sure wouldn't tell you two to watch it if it wasn't for real. Maybe this is how she got to be so famous. Maybe one day she woke up and decide that she wanted to be a model and actress and then focused on that every day like they did in the movie. Maybe we're supposed to decide what we want to be and what we want in life and then somehow it will happen. Does that make sense?" she asked. "Like, I've been wanting a new piano for a while now, so if I focus on that for the next few weeks or a month maybe I will get one too, just like the movie said."

"That makes sense. Do you guys want to go outside and make those boards like they did in the movie? Remember, where they drew pictures or cut them out of things they wanted? Then we can hang them up in the play room where they won't get wrecked," I offered.

"Yeah!" Demi exclaimed. "I'll go get the markers and paper and I can bring them downstairs. Um," she paused. "Do you think we should get out of our jammies before we go outside though?" she giggled. "I don't think I should wear my nighty outside in the grass."

After agreeing that it would be better if we were dressed before heading outside, we changed and chattered about what supplies we would need for our project. Taking what we needed, we headed out to the small hill behind our house.

"What are you going to draw first, Miranda?" Demi asked once we had set up our coloring station on the hill.

We may have brought a bit much outside, I thought, after looking at our pile of supplies. Crayons, markers, stationery paper, stickers, glitter, my new geometry set from school, rulers, glue sticks, and some of moms' old magazines she gave us a few months ago littered the ground around us.

After some thought Miranda replied, "Well, first thing I think I will draw is my piano. I've been wanting it for a while now so I will draw that and then maybe a dress that I saw at the mall a while ago when I was shopping with my mom. What about you guys? Amber, what are you going to draw?"

"Well, since Christmas I've been wanting this Flutterbye fairy doll, the one with light up wings. I saw it in the Christmas catalogue and begged mom for it and even wrote to Santa asking for it but didn't get it. So, I'm going to draw it here and hopefully I get it this year. That, and an Easy-Bake oven, so I can make all the cookies and treats I want. Oh, and maybe some new princess dress up clothes."

"Maybe you can make us some cookies and cakes too! Oh, we could have a baking party! Yeah, you should draw that. Dix, what about you?" Miranda asked next.

"Well," I stop to think about what I wanted to draw. "If I could have anything in the world, I think it would be the new career of the year Barbie and a gold necklace with a letter "D" or a heart on it. I like jewelry a lot and it would be nice to have a real gold one. I would also like some walkie-talkies for me and Demi, to use when we play around the house. Oh, and some new note books so I can write stories and a laptop so I can make good copies of my work. I really like to make my own stories up, so maybe if I can make good copies, I can turn them into a book!" I explain with excitement. "What about you, Dem? I bet I know what you want. You probably want a princess tent and make-up strand like you circled in the catalogue, don't you?"

She smirked and looked up from what she had already started to draw and color. "Oh, yeah, I'm definitely going to draw both of those, but first I am drawing a camera. The kind where you can take a picture and then it pops out the bottom. This way I can practice being a model like Aunty. You can take the pictures and I can pose by the flowers and in our playroom in aunties clothes. And then maybe you can help me put them together and make a...what's that thing aunty showed us of hers before? The folder with her pictures in them."

"Her portfolio?" I asked.

"Yeah, do you think we could make one if this stuff really works and I somehow get a camera?"

I smiled at her; she was determined to be just like Aunt Lisa one day.

"Yeah, for sure."

We then got down to business and began drawing all the material things we could ever want. We sat in silence for probably close to twenty minutes as we drew every detail needed.

"So, they said that in order for this to work, the best thing to do is visualize and pretend that we already have it. So, whatever we draw we have to then pretend that we already have it in our hands."

Everyone stared at me with a blank expression on their faces. "Miranda, you drew a piano, right? So now that you know what it looks like, you pretend it's in front of you and you can play it."

"Like this?" Miranda asked as she smiled, rolled up her sleeves and played her air piano.

"Exactly!" I exclaim. "And Demi, you pretend to put on your make up at your make up stand and pretend to take pictures with your camera. Amber, you pretend to play with your fairy doll like you already got it and maybe act it out what it would be like to get it for Christmas this year. Does that all make sense?" I asked hopefully.

"I get it," Demi said. "Just like you pretend to play

with your Barbie, or use your other Barbies and pretend that they are your career Barbie. Right?" She then held up her hands and told us all to say 'cheese'.

"So, I have an idea. Why don't we all draw out what we want to be when we are older and what kinds of houses and cars we want to drive one day? Maybe even pets that we might want. We have lots of paper."

The next hour was spent, as quiet as four little girls can be expected to be, concentrating on drawing out features of a life we had yet to live.

"Alright guys, I think I'm all done." I stated. "How about all of you? Dem, you finished?"

"Mm-yeah. I think so. I just have one more thing…and there. Yep, I'm finished. Miranda, Amber? How about you? I can't wait to see everyone's pictures." Amber and Miranda then grinned at each other.

"Yeah, we are done."

"Perfect," I exclaimed. "Now, why don't we count to three and then we turn our pictures around and show each other what they are all at the same time? Demi can go first and we will go in a circle. So, it will be Demi, then Amber, Miranda, and then me. Okay ready?" Each of us picked up our papers and held them on our laps. "One-two-THREE!" We then all flipped over our pictures and looked around both excited and curious as to what the others had drawn. "Okay, Dem, do you want to start? We already know what you want to be when you get big but show us what you drew and what other things you want."

Demi beamed with pride and began explaining her picture.

"Okay, well, here in the middle I drew me as a model because I want to be that so much when I grow up. See how long my hair is and my nails are painted. So, that's what I want to be, and then this is the house I want to have. It a real big one. And my car is a limousine because that's what models drive around in."

"What's that?" Miranda asked. "In the top right corner."

"Oh, this? This is a naked cat with a pink glitter necklace. Her name is Gigi McNotfuzzles. Get it? Because she's not fuzzy." She then began to giggle once again.

We all joined in and laughed when Amber asked "Why Gigi though? And why does it have to be naked? Aren't those funny looking?"

"Because, she's a model. Mom sometimes watches a show about rich housewives and one lady has a really pretty daughter named Gigi who is a model now. So, I'm going to name my kitty after her and I want a naked cat because only rich people own them. I'm going to be rich and a model so it only makes sense."

I shook my head and giggled to myself. Demi has such expensive taste, but at the same time, so do I. "Alright, Demi if you're are done, its Amber's turn." Amber then picked up her paper with a smile.

"Okay well, first off I decided that I am going to be a fancy hotel owner. I'm going to have lots of hotels all over the country with different special rooms and pretty chocolates on peoples' pillows. My parents were talking about some fancy hotels last time daddy went on one of his business trips and they said that the owners must be lucky because they probably make lots of money. So, that's what I'm going to be. This is a picture of one of the hotels. And then here is my house. It's a big white one that looks like the White House. See the pillars? And then over here I decided that I am going to drive one of those punch beetles. A nice red one. I like to think they look like lady bugs. Oh, and I'm going to have a dog named Jasmine, like off Aladdin. What did you draw Miranda?"

We then turn to Miranda and her drawing. "Well, I couldn't decide what I want to be so I chose either a pianist or a doctor. I really want to play the piano and think it would be super fun to play in front of lots of people. Also, I would like to be a doctor so I can save people's lives. So, I drew me playing the piano and then beside it I drew me doing surgery. Then I drew the car I want. I want a nice white Mercedes like my mom has. She sells this stuff called Arbonne and she won her car a few years ago because she sold so much and I really like her car so I want one too. My house is going to be a log cabin because I think they are cool. So, I drew that down here. I will also have three horses and two bunny rabbits and maybe a parrot."

"Oh, I love horses," Amber exclaimed. "Can I come ride them with you one day?"

"Yeah sure." Miranda replied. "Alright, Dixie. It's your turn. What do you want to be and what kind of house do you want to live in?"

"Yeah, Dix what do you want to have?" Demi asked excitedly.

I picked my paper from my lap and held it up for all three to see.

"So, after thinking really hard about what I want to be I decided that I for sure want to be a writer. I love books and want to write my own best sellers like the *Harry Potter* books. So, I drew myself holding my first ever published book. See? I think I want to live in Toronto when I get older because that's probably where people publish books. I drew the Toronto sign right here and I also drew a nice big house in the city…This right here, is the guy I'll probably marry one day. He is my soul mate and is going to have brown hair, blue eyes and will be six feet tall. So, I drew him standing next to me. And then my car is going to be a Bentley. I saw one in a magazine once. I don't want any pets because I don't think I want any in the city and they are too much work. So, yeah, that's what I decided on. Maybe in time I will add more, but I think for now this will be a good start." I finally pause and looked at everyone else as they sat in silence.

"Those are all really good dreams Dixie, but won't you miss us here? If you leave and go that far away we won't ever be able to see you," Miranda quietly asked.

"Well, I will come home sometimes, and then we will hang out just like we are now. Either way, it's a long time from now and we don't even know if this stuff works yet so let's not worry about that part, okay?"

Miranda looked at me for a moment, then nodded. Just as Demi was about to say something, Dad called us for lunch.

"Be right there, Dad!" I yelled from the back yard. "So should we hang these in the play room? We can do that after lunch and after we put all of the colouring supplies away."

"Yeah I think we should," Demi agreed. "Hey look over there, by the sandbox." We turned to see what Demi had discovered. "Dandelions! Let's make wishes when we go in."

"Okay," I said as we hurriedly picked up all our things and headed towards the rather sad little patch of dandelions that was growing beside the sandbox. We each picked one and prepared to make our wishes.

"I wish for my piano," Miranda said, closing her eyes as she blew her dandelion away.

"I wish to be a model and for my camera," Demi said firmly, took a big breath and blew as hard as she could.

"I wish for my Flutterbye and an Easy Bake Oven," Amber wished next and blew her seeds into the air.

"Girls! Come on, pizza's getting cold!" Dad shouted from the house.

The others all ran towards the house, without realizing that I had yet to make my wish.

"I wish for this to be real, for us to be able to wish for what we want and get it," I whispered, then looked at my picture once more before closing my eyes and blowing my dandelion puff into the gentle breeze.

Chapter Four

"Alright, so after you put all the linens away we will head down and see if anyone needs help prepping dinner. If no one needs help there, we will take a coffee break, sound good?" I asked Demi as we finished folding sheets from the dryer and tucking them away on the shelf before heading towards the kitchen on the main floor.

"Sounds great!" she replied cheerfully. "You said there's a new coffee machine here, right? I'm looking forward to that."

It was Demi's first day working at the retirement home in town. I have been working here since the end of the ninth grade and I must say that I absolutely love it.

The retirement home has, in a way, become like a second home for me. Growing up, I didn't fit in with the rest of the kids in my class aside from Miranda, Amber and, of course, Demi, even though she was younger than me. I was always a book lover and not as outgoing as most kids my age. I didn't like to party or play many sports for that matter, and I never understood the point in pulling pranks or dealing with drama like everyone else in my class. I always preferred to stay home, study hard, read as well as write books. I had researched everything possible when it came to writing and publishing one's own stories and when I got this job, I realized how much I loved to go there to work. I guess you could say that I was an outcast in school but going to the retirement home after school hours and on the weekends felt like a safe place for me. A place where no one would judge me for my love for books and studying the way that I did. A place where everyone was an adult and knew how to get along and laugh, joke, and love one another no matter who you were. I felt...safe and cared for. It felt like another home to me, which explains why I was going to miss the place when I would leave for Toronto at the end of the following summer.

Luckily, I could get Demi a job before I went, so this way she could take my place and I'll know that residents were in good hands.

Growing up, Demi had been a lovable goof and very driven, much like myself. She has always been more outgoing than me and into anything that could potentially make her the center of attention. She excelled at sports, unlike myself, and she had that something about her much like Aunt Lisa did, where everyone loved her just because of her glowing personality. The residents happen to love people who can bring life to this place, which explains why they would love her just as much.

The best part about working at the retirement home was that I didn't have one particular area that I worked in, and neither would Demi. Our position was called the "floater" position. One day we could be doing laundry, whereas the next we could be helping in the kitchen or working on new activities to keep the residents active and entertained. It's great because it's almost impossible to get bored, not to mention that the residents and other staff members are a lot of fun.

I have developed a wonderful friendship with one elderly woman here, Thelma. She is in her mid-eighties and full of life as well as stories. She had lost her husband over thirty years ago, and, after her grieving period was over, she decided to find other women in her same situation and talk them into traveling the world with her. She travelled for the next ten years off and on and had seen things that a person could only ever dream of. She truly is a remarkable person and I couldn't wait to introduce Demi to her.

The other person I wanted Demi to meet was Lori. Lori used to be one of our mother's friends before we lost Aunt Lisa and Mom changed. Lori is one of the managers at the facility, and when I applied four years ago, she knew exactly who I was, and offered me the position. She's full of life and tries not to take things too seriously, kind of like Mom used to be.

There are so many great people here, so many people with different stories and experiences and all willing to share those experiences, if only they are asked. I know that Demi will be okay here, and I know that I can leave these people knowing that she's here for them, too.

"Do you guys need help today?" I asked automatically as I entered the kitchen, Demi on my heels.

Andrea and Gabby were working. Gabby tiptoed to look over the island in the kitchen whilst adjusting her hairnet over top of her barely contained grey curls, her blue eyes twinkling. I've always liked the head cook here, mostly because when I first started she used to sneak me brownies on Thursdays when she made them for dessert for the residents.

"Today is training day and this is my sister Demi; you can call her Dem if you want."

Demi smiled and said 'hello' with a small wave in their direction.

"Do you need help?" I asked a second time. "Salads prepped, dessert topped?"

"No dear, I think we are fine," Andrea smiled cheerfully, wiping her hands on her apron as she walked around the corner from the sink. "Thank you, but we got everything done early today. So, this is the wondrous Demi that we have heard so much about. I'm Andrea, if you ever need anything make sure to let me know and just a heads up, the kitchen is the best place in the whole building to work mostly because you get to work with us and well…we're awesome here."

Andrea was normally the most outgoing here at the retirement home. She had a laugh that would ring in your ears, but also had the biggest heart you could imagine. She had medium length blonde hair that she always had tied up in a hair net. She had the most beautiful blue eyes that hid behind a pair of thick framed glasses and wasn't overly tall but wasn't the shortest in the room either. Gabby wins for the shortest. Andrea was thirty years old, but definitely a kid at heart.

"And I'm Gabby. Don't listen to anything Andrea says. She will get you into trouble. Trouble should actually be her middle name," she smirked and winked towards Andrea. Gabby was approximately sixty-five with a petite frame which had her barely hit the five-foot mark. "We are the heads of the kitchen, so when it comes to working in here or the dining room you come to Andrea or myself for questions. Sound good?"

"Yes, Ma'am," Demi replied with a quick smile that made adults believe anything she said. "How long have you both been working here?"

Andrea and Gabby looked at one another.

"Well, Gabby here has been working what? Ten years and I have been here eight." Andrea piped up. "We both look forward to many more years ahead of us. You'll understand once you get into the groove of things and how everything works. We all become one big family, so when one of us leaves it's like a little piece of us leaves. Isn't that right, Dixie?" She then looked over at me with a very direct look and I smiled and put my head down slightly, knowing she was, again, telling me I would be missed.

"Yeah, yeah I know," I looked up again. "But I'm going to miss you guys as well. You've been my life other than school and home for the past three years. It won't be easy leaving, believe me. I will likely be coming back more often than you all think and when I do I'll be expecting some of your famous orange glazed chicken and key lime parfaits."

"I expect regular visits, then," Gabby responded cheerfully as she looked up at the clock. "Well, you girls better get going for your break if you were wanting one. Lunch is in half an hour and we have a bit of tidying left to do. We will talk again soon."

"Ready to go try that new coffee machine I was

telling you about?" I asked Demi, but then looked at Andrea and smiled, "I hear someone brought some of my favorite raspberry syrup to add to it if you'd like."

"Sure, I could use a coffee right about now. It was a pleasure meeting you ladies and I look forward to working with you."

"Wait, before you go, try one of these," Andrea handed us each a thick slice of coconut cream pie from where she was placing it in preparation for lunch. "Remember Demi, this is the fun place." She winked and got back to her kitchen duties.

We walked down the hallway and into the employee break room where we set our pie on the table.

"They seem really nice. Is Andrea always that cheery?" Demi asked. "And did they made these from scratch? How is that even possible? They look incredible."

"Yeah, she's a pretty happy person. You'll learn a lot from her. Sometimes a bit more than you were hoping to…" I trail off with fond memories of some of Andrea's inappropriate jokes and stories.

"What do you mean? More than I hope to?"

"You'll find out," I smirk to myself. "Alright, so this is the new coffee maker. You can have French vanilla, hot chocolate, Irish cream, a mocha or over here you can have regular coffee," I point to the old coffee maker sitting beside the new one.

"I'll try a French vanilla. It's been a long time since I've had one of those," Demi said, sitting down. "Thanks."

After a few moments of silence as we took our first sips, Demi spoke again.

"So they all seem pretty sad that you are leaving in the fall. Do you think you will really miss them and this place as much as you think?"

I thought about it for a minute before answering.

"You know, when I first started here, I didn't think much about it other than it would be a way to make some money. But, as time went on and I got to know the workers and residents, I realized that I actually will miss them. Like Andrea said, we are like family here. Whether it's the workers or the residents." I paused briefly. "The one person I think I will miss the most is Thelma."

"Is she one of the residents? The one you said travelled lots?" Demi leaned forward, placing her mug on the table.

"Yes. I swear she's one of my best friends, other than you, Miranda and Amber. We clicked right off the bat and, honestly, I feel like I can tell her anything. She's so knowledgeable and understanding. Any time I've ever had a rough time at school and kids poked and prodded at me for my love of books and studying, she was the one who always knew what to say to make me feel better. She's one of those people who can comfort anyone at any given time. I think you will really like her."

"I'm sure I will. I like all of the same kind of people that you like," Demi hesitated before continuing. "But on the topic of you leaving, clearly I'm all for it and rooting for you. I think you'll have so much fun and do really well in life, but…um, have you mentioned this to Miranda and Amber yet? I mean, how do you think they will take it?"

It was then my turn to hesitate as I began to bite my lower lip nervously. "I haven't said a word to them yet. Honestly, I'm not sure they will be as supportive as you, and Mom and Dad have been. I mean, I know they want me to be happy and do well, but… you know them, they aren't as open minded as you and I. They're okay with the little things, they don't strive to accomplish more than what's in front of them. Know what I mean? Truthfully, I'm kind of scared to tell them."

But you realize that you should, sooner than later, right? Summer only lasts a few months and I think that, if you tell them now, it will give them time to think about it and hopefully be a bit more supportive than you think they will be. You know, I'd be upset if you waited until the last minute to tell me something so important. I think that you kind of owe it to them as they are our best friends."

I thought about what Demi just said to me and realized that she was right. "Okay, I'll tell them tonight, when we are at the campground. Then I can get it out in the open and you'll be there so you can back me if I need you to."

"Absolutely." She lifted her mug again, taking a sip of her French vanilla. "I think you're paranoid, though, don't you remember 'what you think about most, you will create?' I'm sure that they will be easier on you than you believe. They are our friends and we've known them for forever, surely they want you to go and do great things. I know I do. Besides, this way, when I graduate, I will have a place to stay until I get my modeling underway," she smirked.

"Oh thanks, so you will use me for my place. You're so supportive," we both grinned at each other for a moment before I glanced up at the clock. "Well, break time is about up. We need to head upstairs to meet Thelma. We may even meet Lori along the way. You met Kathy the other day, but Lori is the other manager, and I know she's dying to meet you."

"Sounds perfect," Demi replied, slurping the last of her drink and eyeing the pie that had a single bite from it. Demi was nothing if not determined.

We took our time heading upstairs to the residents' area, Demi examining the paintings on the wall as we walked.

"These are really pretty; I wish I could paint like this," she said scrutinizing a landscape.

"Me, too," I agreed. "Some of the residents painted these. My favorite one is in the lobby. One lady painted a piano with a vase filled with pink roses. The detail will blow your mind."

We approached room eighty-four, where the door stood ajar. Thelma always enjoyed company, and she often left the door slightly cracked so people knew to stop in whenever they liked without having to knock. Despite this, old habits die hard and I always knocked anyhow.

"Come in. Oh, hello there!" Thelma exclaimed when I pushed the door open. "Well, look what the wind blew in! Dear, I haven't seen you in almost a week! How are you?" I pushed the door fully open and walked inside with Demi not far behind. "Oh, and you have a friend." Thelma then looked Demi up and down pausing at her face.

"No, wait, that's not just a friend. This must be Demi. The Demi that I hear so many wonderful things about."

Demi smiled once more. Even Demi can't smile so much in one day, and I begin to wonder if her cheeks are starting to get sore yet.

"And this must be the wonderful Thelma that *I* hear so much about. It really is a pleasure to meet you. Dixie has told me so much about you and many of your life experiences. It is nice to finally meet you in person."

"Likewise, my dear. Come, both of you have a seat. I have some hot water ready, I just poured myself a cup of tea. Would you like some?"

"You know, Thelma," I replied as we sat on the couch beside one another. "We actually just had a coffee downstairs but thank you, anyway. We just stopped in so I could introduce the two of you. Demi will be working here and taking my place shortly. I thought you two would like to meet before I head off."

"Well, I appreciate that very much, and it is a pleasure to meet you. I hope your sister here doesn't get you into too much trouble."

"Me, too, she always had a way of getting me into certain predicaments. Isn't that right, Dix?"

"Oh come on, I got you into trouble, like, what…five times growing up?"

"HA! Sure, we'll go with that," she then turned to Thelma. "She did a lot more than I'm sure she has ever mentioned to you."

"Oh, I believe that. That's what big sisters are for," Thelma winked and looked in my direction. "Now dear, have you got all of your things packed yet?"

I crossed my legs and leaned back. "Not yet, I still have the rest of the summer to get things ready and organized. I don't want to pack everything too soon and then have to sift through boxes for the next three months until I go. Or what? Are you trying to get rid of me already?" I jokingly question.

"Well…" she beamed.

I pretend to get off the couch.

"Now, now," Thelma leaned forward to pat my hand. "You know I'm going to miss you."

"No drama necessary, Dixie," Demi laughed, then winked at Thelma. I knew they'd get along, and it made me a little less sad about leaving to see that I wasn't leaving Thelma, or Demi, alone.

Shaking my head, I sat back down, "Joking aside, no, I'm not ready yet. I feel like I have a lot to do before the end of summer."

"Such as tell your friends?" Demi threw in.

I froze in my spot, eyes wide as saucers and began to bite my lip once again as I glance at Thelma. I then smile a very awkward smile.

"You mean you haven't told the other girls yet? Dixie! Why haven't you told your friends?" She asked with a tone my own grandmother would have used. "You do realize they will find out sooner or later and the longer you hold off on telling them, the more hurt they will be?"

"Yeah, I understand, only I really don't think they will be as supportive as everyone else is. I mean, I was telling Demi earlier… they aren't the types that are willing to let things go. They hold onto this simple, small town life and aren't willing to try things out of this town like I am. I feel like I need to go out and at least try to publish my books. I need to try to further my life beyond this," I open my arms. "Don't get me wrong, I do love it here and Moville will always be my home, but I need to expand, kind of like you and how you travelled to so many interesting places. You saw what was out there and then you found your nesting ground. I need to do that, too, and I don't think that Miranda and Amber will understand. I don't think anyone other than you guys and my parents will ever fully understand. Well, you all and Grandma Marg, of course."

"You know, Dixie," Thelma's tone became serious. "You will never know how people will respond unless you tell them, and being afraid doesn't help any situation. By holding off you will only make the situation worse. So, I recommend putting on your big girl panties and doing what you know needs to be done. I have known you for, what? Three to four years now, and the Dixie I know isn't scared of anything. If these girls are your true friends, I believe that they will find it in their hearts to be truly happy for you and, if not, then you need to ask yourself if they are your true friends. Because a true friend will be by your side and support the heck out of you, no matter what direction you choose in life. You see your sister here? She is honestly happy for you, isn't she?"

Demi nodded.

"So right here, you have not only a sister, but you have a friend, and this is what you are looking for in those girls. If they can't be supportive, then they are the ones to suffer, not you. You don't need that kind of negativity when you are trying to find your place in this world.

"Hun, if I could give you any more words of advice other than to stay true to yourself, it would be to smile. Even if telling the girls doesn't go as planned, by keeping a smile on that pretty little face of yours you will find a way to be happy regardless. My mother always told me that if you can fake a smile long enough, it will eventually turn into a real one. And you know what? It has worked for me time and time again, so I know it will work for you. You are a strong, young woman and I don't want to see you give up your life dreams just because someone might not be happy with the life you choose. If those girls want to stay here and continue to live the life they are living, then that's their decision. You are a grown woman and are able to decide for yourself what you want to do with your own life."

I sat back into the couch and let Thelma's words process as I continue to bite my lower lip. "You know what? You're right. This is my life and I have the right to do what I want. You are happy for me, Demi is happy for me, my parents are happy for me, and so is everyone else who works here. So, why wouldn't they be happy, too?" I look over at Thelma and then back at Demi. "You know what? I'm going to tell them. I will tell them tonight, for sure, and if they can't support me then they aren't the people I thought they were. Thank you. I really needed this."

At that moment, the intercom, wired into each resident's room and throughout the hallways, crackled to life, a scratchy version of Gabby's voice announcing dinner being served in the residents' dining room.

"See?" Thelma pushed the button on the arm of her chair and was lifted gracefully to her feet. "I knew that the Dixie I knew was in there somewhere…"

The rest of the way down the dining room, Thelma explained to Demi and me her determination to sit with the three elderly gentlemen who always sat at a corner table together. Mack, Jack, and Joe were well-loved and much sought after in the small residential community as canasta partners, and Thelma explained that sitting with them was desirous because, "they're a lot more entertaining that those crusty old women! And besides, they let me in on their poker games."

As we left her at her table of choice, Demi patted her on the shoulder, "It was lovely to meet you, Thelma."

"You, too, my dear. As I said, keep me posted," she winked and turned to the men, teasing Joe about the beard he recently showed off.

Demi glanced in my direction as we walked side by side. "You're still scared, aren't you, Dix?"

I look back at her with fear written all over my face. "More than you know."

Chapter Five

"Oh my gosh, you guys, this weekend is going to be so much fun!" Amber began to unpack her bag as we all got settled into the yurt that we had rented for the weekend. "School is out. *Forever*, we are officially at *drinking age* and I must say that this is going to be, by far, the best summer ever. Don't you guys think so?"

We all glanced at one another and agreed that it would be wonderful. "Yeah, now if only I graduated, too, and was able to drink with you guys it would be perfect. So, while you all get tipsy, I'll get to babysit your butts." Demi dead-panned. "Just remember, whatever you do or say can and will be held against you."

Through the laughter, teasing and getting in each other's way, we finally managed to get ourselves sorted out and organized, ready for the weekend we had been promising ourselves since the eleventh grade.

"Where is the ice?" Amber called from the kitchenette. "Miranda, don't tell me you forgot to bring ice!"

"Okay," said Miranda, shrugging as she continued to tuck sheets onto her bunk.

"How am I supposed to make margaritas without ice? And I intend to make margaritas!" Amber, her love of sweets and caloric indulgences made all the more obvious by her plump hips and ample curves.

"I'm sure there is ice at the Fort," Miranda stated, pushing her empty bag underneath her bed.

Miranda always did enjoy being in charge. Since her parents had a set of twins after she turned nine, she stepped up to become a leader. "And then we can roast some wieners and make some waffle cone s'mores. Maybe after that we can go for a swim, seeing as the lake is right here and we don't have far to walk."

"I'm too tired to swim tonight," I said, "but I'm happy to sit around a fire and stuff myself with marshmallows."

Miranda gave me a disgruntled look, but I really didn't want to swim, and if I was going to take this opportunity to tell them my future plans, Miranda was going to have to get used to not being in charge of everything we did. Besides, if the others wanted to, they were free to go; we didn't always have to do everything together.

"If you and Dixie start the fire," Amber said. "Demi and I will go get some ice."

Within minutes, Amber and Demi were gone, and Miranda was carrying wood from the woodpile to the fire pit. I started making kindling using the small axe we had brought along while she went back for another load.

"I love this time of the year, don't you, Dix? I mean, the fresh air, the camping, no rules and endless days of enjoying ourselves. Summer is definitely my recharge time. What's your favorite part of summer?"

I thought about it for a moment. I hadn't been thinking fully since deciding to tell the girls my news. I had been rather quiet so far, actually.

"I think that my favorite part is the sunshine and the greenness. Everything is alive and fresh, beginning again. I do enjoy the fresh air, as well. I mean, the air is warm and welcoming, not like the winter when it's so cold and you freeze when you go outside. I can actually sit outdoors and read or write in peace. Getting a tan is a bonus." I finished chopping the wood and attempted to light the fire.

"This really is great, and to top it off we all get to be together. Like sure, we have jobs and everything but for the most part, knowing that we can have a few days a week to just chill, it's awesome. I agree with Amber. I think this will be our best summer yet."

I kept my head down so Miranda wouldn't see the discouragement in my eyes, knowing I won't be here as long as she thinks.

"Seeing as we are drinking age, I brought us all something," Miranda ran back into the yurt and came out with a plastic bag filled with tumbler cups. "I got us each one of these!" She was clearly excited. "I got us all a different color so we don't get them mixed up." In her arms were four brightly colored lidded cups, decorated with bright rhinestones. Handing me the green one, she grinned.

"Yours is green," her eyes sparkled with excitement. "See? I did your name in rhinestones. Mine's red."

I notice there are purple and pink, clearly for Amber and Demi. They're pretty and I thanked her.

"Thanks, I love it," I smiled. Thinking of all the times Miranda had organized us, set the stage for our adventures, and made everything just a little more enjoyable with her preparations.

"Shall we test them out…?" she asked, just as the others arrived back, arms full of supplies.

"We got the ice, but we also got a few bottles of mix because I forgot to grab some when we left the house," Amber chimed. "Hey, what are those?" She nodded towards the cups sitting on the table.

"Hey! Those are awesome. Where did you get these?" Demi picked up the pink one with her name to examine it.

"I bought the cups while I was in the city the other day and I added our names last night. Be careful that the rhinestones don't fall off. Now that you guys are back, shall we head in to test these puppies out?" Amber headed in with Miranda to get us each a drink while I continued to build up the fire.

"You didn't tell her, did you?" Demi asked quietly when the others were out of ear range.

I looked up to where Demi stood a few feet in front of me. "No. I don't want to ruin the trip on the first night we get here. I think I will wait until the last night before we leave… or maybe forever."

"*Dixie*. You heard what Thelma said. You have to tell them."

"I know, and I will, just not tonight. I want to enjoy this, so I'm going to smile and continue as if nothing is going to happen. They are so excited to finally be here, on this camping trip. Do you really want them to be upset already?"

"Well, no," Demi looked towards the yurt. "I want us all to enjoy this, to be happy."

"Exactly. I promise I will tell them," I assured her. "Just not now."

The yurt door was flung open and Amber called out, "Are you coming with that ice or not?"

"Oh, yeah, sorry!" Demi called back before glancing at me and sighing. "Be right there. And you better only put Sprite in my cup!"

Amber smirked and shook her head before shutting the door again. Because three out of the four of us were of age to consume alcohol, our parents agreed with Demi that the only way she could have alcohol, would be if they were around to supervise, and because it was just us girls, Demi was left to drink alcohol free beverages for the weekend.

"Well, I better get them their ice and make sure that they keep my cup clean. You want Amaretto, right?"

"Please, but not too strong," Demi then headed inside not looking back once.

The next day came too quickly. I was the first to wake up just before six. After slowly getting out of bed, I quietly retreated outside with the coffee maker and tin of coffee grounds. Looking around blankly, I realized that the only electrical outlet was right beside the door, and the smell of coffee, not to mention the noise of making it, was probably going to wake the others.

There was not much better than a good cup of coffee as you watch the morning dawn. I've always loved the early morning, the quiet and the solitude of it, the sounds as birds came alive, and the breeze rustling leaves…it's a special time of the day, and I find it soothing.

Surprisingly, I managed to brew the pot without hearing the sound of anyone stirring from inside the yurt. I filled my travel mug and decided to take a short walk to look at the view from a few camp sites over.

The air was fresh and crisp, and there was a fine dew that covered the ground. This has always been one of my favorite times of the day. Mainly, because the world was so still. Today, however, there happened to be a handful of birds and a trio of squirrels that ran out in front of me and into the bushes along the path. Everything was peaceful, soothing and perfect.

I quietly continued down the path until I came to an opening around the corner where I found a fenced drop off to the valley below. There was a bench, and I decided to sit down and drink my coffee. Watching as the sun slowly crept its way up into the sky I saw a handful of deer grazing for their breakfast at the bottom of the valley, across the river that ran through the valley bottom. I had probably sat there for a good forty-five minutes, sipping my coffee and enjoying the world waking around me when I heard footsteps behind me.

"Beautiful morning, isn't it?"

I turned around to see who it was and paused when I saw that the person speaking to me had to be, by far, the most attractive man I have ever seen in my life. He clearly wasn't from around here. I would most certainly have known him if he were, and I would not have forgotten him if I knew him. Light brown hair was still mess, not having seen a comb yet this morning. Strangely, it appeared he had taken the time to shave, because there was no stubble showing, and the clothes screamed 'city'.

No, he definitely wasn't from small-town Moville. Just before it became awkward, I caught myself staring and, taking a breath I responded.

"Yes," I said. "It's gorgeous." I blushed. How much

more inane could I possibly have been. Gorgeous? I blushed, and turned back to look out on the valley before he could see my bright red face. As I did so, he approached to stand beside me.

"Mind if I sit?" He gestured with the hand that held his own mug.

"Um, yeah, sure," I fought to get my words out. *Why am I acting like this? It's not like I've never seen a man before.*

"Come on Dix, get a grip on yourself," I thought to myself as he took a seat next to me.

"It's a bit early to be up, don't you think? You always get up so early?"

I looked at him in the eyes and hesitated for a brief second.

"It's not too early," I continued to look out at the valley. "I mean, yes, I usually am a bit of an early bird, but I enjoy the fresh and quiet mornings before the rest of the world gets up. It gives me time to think and plan my day. Why? Are you normally up this early, too? I don't see many faces this often as the sun is coming up."

"Yeah, I definitely am," He stretched his legs out and leaned back into the bench, coffee resting on his leg. "Same reasons. I like to think and enjoy the quiet. Not too many people my age are morning people, but me, I prefer to get up and get my day started as soon as possible. You only live once, right?"

I agreed with him and we sat in silence for a moment, just staring out at the view that I had been admiring for the past hour by myself.

"My name's Turner by the way," I looked over at him as he stuck his hand out while staring me in the eyes.

I lightly smiled, took his hand and shook it firmly. He had a nice firm grip.

"Dixie," I replied. "It's a pleasure to meet you."

He smiled back with a twinkle in his eye. "Pleasure's all mine. So, are you from around here, or just visiting?"

"Oh, I'm from here. Born and raised, actually. I'm

here to kick off my last summer with my sister and two best friends."

"Sounds great, why is this your last summer? Are you going away to school or something?"

"No, not to school, *perse,* more like just leaving to find a life of my own. Away from here."

"I see. What's wrong with here? This is a quaint little town, isn't it? I mean, I've come here the past three summers and it seems decent enough. There seem to be a lot of small businesses-" I sat in silence with a blank expression on my face. "But, you need more. I understand."

"Yes, it's not like the town itself isn't great. I mean, the people are nice enough and everything, only I want to know what else is out there, and if I don't find anything then maybe my compass will point back here, but for now I'm going to head out and try to discover something new. Know what I mean?"

"Yeah… I do," He stared at me for a long moment.

"So, you never told me whe-" Suddenly, we heard a few giggles and my name being called from a short way into the trail that I came out of myself. When I turned around I found Demi, Miranda, and Amber walking out towards us. "Well, good morning you bunch of sleepy heads. I thought it was you that I heard coming." I smile a welcoming smile towards the girls.

"Good morning to you…*two*… Who's your friend, Dix?" Miranda tilted her head as she stepped up beside me and began playing with my hair.

"Oh. This is, um, Turner," I looked over nervously at him. "Turner, these are my friends, Amber and Miranda, and this is my sister, Demi."

He nodded and raised a hand in greeting. "Pleasure." His voice was mesmerizing. "Dixie was just telling me that you are all here to start your summer off? Well, a bunch of us guys and I are all doing the same thing. If you want, we are planning a bonfire later tonight if you'd like to stop in."

All four of us girls glanced at one another and silently agreed to the invitation.

"I think that would be a lot of fun," I turned back toward him. "Where are you guys staying?"

"We are in bay seven, lot two. Party should start around six or seven, whenever you ladies show up, really."

"We'll see you then. Can't wait to meet everyone," Amber then chimed, "Are you girls ready to go for breakfast? I'm starving and could go for one of the Forts famous bacon and egg omelets. Dix, you ready?"

"Actually," I looked back at Turner. "I am kind of hungry, it was really nice meeting you. Maybe we can talk some more tonight?'

He looked me in the eyes once again. I swear, if he keeps doing this I am going to lose my mind.

"Absolutely. I look forward to it. You girls have a great day now and we will talk soon."

Nodding, I somehow managed to get back on the path and back to our camp site without tripping.

"Who on God's green earth was that and *how* did you meet him?" Demi hissed at me in an undertone as we approached the yurt. "He has to be the most beautiful thing I have ever seen in my life."

"Yeah missy, I thought we all agreed way back when that there was a no hoarding policy on the hotties," Miranda threw in.

"Spill," Amber demanded next, succinct as always.

"Okay, first of all, while you lazy bums were still sleeping I got up and made coffee; you're welcome by the way; and decided to go for a walk. You know, to enjoy the sun-rise and wake up. Well, I went to the drop off where I watched a bunch of deer eat and as I was about to get up and come back, this guy randomly walked up behind me and started talking about how pretty the morning was and introduced himself. Then, you guys walked it. It's nothing, really."

"Oh, my God, Dixie. He was totally into you!"

Miranda exclaimed. "No guy sits down and talks about the sun if he isn't *into* you."

"She's blushing!" Amber taunted.

"I am not," I tried to fight back but I knew then that I was, indeed, blushing and there was no point at all in trying to argue the fact. Just thinking about those eyes had me turning redder by the second. "And he was not *into* me, Miranda. We were just talking. I was sitting alone so he decided to be polite and have a grown-up conversation while sitting beside me. I don't see the big deal. Anyway, I need to grab my purse from inside, I kind of need money if we are going for breakfast."

I reached for the door and walked inside while the girls followed suit. Just then I realized that I was still in my pyjamas. I could face-palm myself so hard right now. I just talked to the most attractive man on Earth and I am wearing my flip flops, flannel pyjama pants and an old ratty tank top, not to mention my hair, in a greasy messy bun atop my head. *Crap.*

"He was totally into her and it's so obvious. Why else do you think he invited us for a bonfire, Dixie? Just because he was being *polite*? Yeah, I don't think so," Demi looked at all three of us wide eyed. "Oh, my gosh, you guys, if this one was this hot can you *imagine* what his friends must look like? I mean, where there's one, there's more. They come in herds, like you go so long without seeing any good-looking guys and then it's like BAM, they're everywhere. I bet that's what's going to happen. Guys this handsome don't travel alone."

"You're all insane," I shake my head. "Certifiable. You all need help. And I need food. I'm going to get ready, then I'm heading down for breakfast. If anyone wants to join me, rather than speculate on those in the surrounding camp sites, I'd be happy to have you along."

With this, we all slowly washed and changed. I also figured out something to do with my hair. Not because Tuner might be at breakfast. No, absolutely not.

Chapter Six

The day went by surprisingly quickly. After breakfast, we changed into our swimsuits and headed down to the beach for the day. With Amber carrying the snacks and Demi and I both with a blow up under each arm, we headed towards the water. The sun was climbing into the sky, the birds were singing, and kids ran around screaming and laughing everywhere. The temperature had to have been at least twenty degrees Celsius already. It was definitely going to be a hot one, so I was glad that we all decided to stay near the open water of the lake.

"What about over by the tree right their? That looks like a nice place to go," Demi suggested tentatively as we made our way across the blistering sand.

"I think that's a great spot. We'll be partially hidden when the sun gets hotter." I return. "I am so full from breakfast that I don't think I can swim yet. I'm going to lay down for a bit before I go into the water."

"Well, I feel fine so I am going to blow up my swan and head in. This sun is already making me sweat like a beast. Anyone else joining me?" Amber commented.

"I'll come with you," Miranda responded. "I'm already getting warm too, just for a bit, though, then I want to get my brown on and lay here for a few hours. I want an extra dark tan this summer. Demi, are you joining us?"

"Yeah, why not?"

Reaching the tree, we all spread out our towels before Amber, Miranda and Demi blew up their floaty toys and raced towards the water.

I sat down and watched as they raced and dove into the water before coming up screaming about how cold the water was.

"Even more reason to stay up here!" I yelled out and

laughed.

They continued to splash and play as I lay down to enjoy the morning sun. There is something about the beach and listening to the kids and families frolic about that made me really enjoy life right then. Maybe it's the feeling of happiness in the air; I'm not sure, but whatever it is, I like it. I continued to lay there for another twenty minutes or so, people watching, before I dozed off.

Dreaming about Toronto and my books, I had just won an award for my latest work, an autobiography about how I had beat the odds and made a place for myself in that big crazy city, and became an inspiration to others. It had not only become a best seller but it had also made me a six-figure paycheque, which I never imagined would happen as often happens in dreams. I was just at the point of accepting an award when something woke me.

I quickly sat up, startled. "Wha…? Oh, thanks a lot!" I laid back again as the others began to laugh, settling themselves on their own towels around me.

"Good dream, Dixie?" Miranda chuckled. "You've been laying here for two hours. We figured it was time you woke up."

"Two hours? I grabbed my phone, confirming that in fact, just over two hours had passed, and it was now just after eleven o'clock. "Wow, thanks for waking me. I can't believe I slept that long!" Stretching luxuriously, I consider the possibility of heading into the water for a wake-up.

"The excitement of meeting Turner must have tuckered you out," Amber smirked, adjusting her sunglasses on her nose. She was slathered with lotion, and her hair was pulled tightly up and under a floppy-brimmed hat.

"Ha-ha, you are so funny," I stuck my tongue out at her. "So, how was your swim? It couldn't have been too cold if you guys were in the water for *two* hours."

"It was nice. You got used to it relatively quickly. They cleaned it up nice since the flood last year. There's no gooey bottom and not really any weeds anymore." Demi looked horrified briefly. "But there are still fish! One touched my foot as I had it hanging off my flamingo floaty. Blah, they're so gross."

"I assume you didn't hear her scream and fall off her bird?" Amber questioned with a laugh.

"Actually, no, I didn't. There's a lot of noise, though, so she probably blended in with everyone else here today. So, what do you guys want to do now? It's almost lunch time and you are probably hungry after all that swimming."

"I'm not quite yet, but I'm sure by the time we pack up, put on some dry clothes and make ourselves presentable, I will be," Miranda said.

"Yes," Demi replied. "Feed me."

The afternoon flew by. Burgers and ice cream for lunch at the fort were worked off by a three-hour hike along the park trails before heading back to the yurt, entertained along the way by Amber and Demi comparing bug bites, for showers and preparing dinner of hot dogs and more of Amber's questionable drink concoctions as the sun began to set.

The day was lovely, and had gone a lot smoother than other similar trips. We hadn't had to run back for things we'd forgotten a dozen times. Or maybe it was just because I hadn't yet told them about my plans.

"So, who's excited to make some new friends tonight?" Miranda asked as we finished up a casual game of lawn darts. "Dixie? How about you? Are you going to give Mister Wonderful your phone number? Or do I have to give him mine?" She teased. "Because you know, he would look pretty darn good hanging off my arm. Just saying."

Miranda always enjoyed picking on me, especially when it came to boys, so I shouldn't have been surprised that she was doing it again. "Miranda, we are hardly even acquaintances, so I don't imagine he is even the slightest bit interested. We talked for, what, a whole ten minutes before you guys came and took me away?" I paused. "However, if, say for some unknown reason, he does ask for my number, then, yes, I will share it with him."

"Now that's the Dixie I was looking for," Amber piped up. "Do you think he will have good looking and decent friends? It feels like forever since I've been on a date."

"That's because it has been forever," teased Demi before suddenly becoming serious. "If we are meant to find someone we will, and if not, then we still have each other, right? This was supposed to be a girl's weekend, anyway. But speaking of boys, it's almost seven o'clock. What do you say we top up cups, pack Amber's bags with supplies, grab me a couple bottles of sparking water, and slowly head towards the party? I can hear music already."

Pausing to listen, we could hear music in the distance.

Upon arriving at the party, we were welcomed with cheers from the group and welcoming arms from none other than Turner himself.

"Welcome ladies." Turner beamed as we walked into the camp site. "We weren't sure if you were going to come, but I'm glad that you decided to join us."

"It's a nice set up you guys have here." Miranda pointed out, looking at the various campers and equipment. "How long are you planning on being here for? Looks like a while."

Turner smiled, "About a month, actually. We all take a month off every summer to come down here to Evergreen Park, clear our heads after a busy school and work year. This is our fun time, I guess you could say."

Miranda liked that answer. She likes men that know how to work but also know how to play. It was very sexy in her eyes.

"Would any of you ladies like a top up on your drinks, by chance?" Turner offered.

"Thanks, I think we're fine," I declined. "But maybe you could introduce us?"

"Of course, how could I be so rude? I, of course am Turner, the tall skinny one over here sitting on the chair by the fire is Logan."

Logan is clearly shy. He seems to be the tallest of the group, and is attractive with dirty blonde hair, bright blue eyes and a charming smile.

"Next to the fire beside Logan is Roland. Careful, those two are crazy when we let them get together."

Roland raised his beer in mock salute, simply greeting us with a "Ladies."

Amber, ever predictable, found herself edging close to the muscular young man.

"And somewhere around here…" Turner looked around, as though searching for something. "Ah, here we go, ladies. Mike, the guy coming out of the camper."

Blonde-haired, blue eyed Mike had not only a huskier build than the others, but a beard as well, and I smirked. He was exactly Miranda's type.

"Now, maybe you ought to introduce yourself to the guys."

Demi poked me in the ribs, making me jump. "Oh, well, I'm Dixie. Behind me here is my sister Demi. This is Miranda, the tall brunette, and on the other side of Miranda is Amber. Thanks for inviting us here tonight."

"Hey, no problem, we just figured rather than spend the evening doing our usual stuff, why not mix it up and make some new friends? Now, why don't you all come, pick a seat by the fire here and make yourselves at home. We have bug spray on the tables, marshmallows and graham crackers inside, and drinks in the coolers and if you don't like beer we have a few mixes inside as well. So please, come, sit and I'm just going to top up because I seem to have gotten a bit low myself."

Tuner pointed towards the open seats by the fire next to Logan, Roland, and Mike, who had just sat down.

We all took a seat and spent the next half hour to forty-five minutes getting to know each other a bit more. Logan is a country boy who apparently is into landscaping and construction, as well as traveling. He seemed to be shy at first but, once he warmed up to us, we discovered that he has an incredible sense of humor, as well as being incredibly genuine and caring. His latest trip involved going to South America for two weeks where he helped design and develop homes in a small village. Along with that, he did some volunteer teaching at a local university.

Turner was a lot like Logan in the sense that they both attended school for landscaping and construction. However, Turner happened to be a bit more of a city guy than Logan. He enjoyed his Starbucks every morning, along with a long run to wake himself up. Hobbies of his included mostly working, but the odd time he would take a hike in a forest nearest to his home. He also planned to start his own business with Logan one day. You could tell how passionate he was with his career choice and, to me, that screamed inspiring. I love when people love what they do for a living, because it shows that they truly enjoy life, rather than living it day to day.

Roland, is pretty funny, too. Anything you say can and will be held against you. He Is a sports junkie who enjoys a good game of football as well as hockey, but that is easy to tell by checking out his fit physique. After talking to him a bit we discovered that he had just finished up his schooling and was on his way to becoming a social worker and is very excited to do so.

Lastly, we have Mike, a kind-hearted and caring guy who is very dedicated to his work. He recently finished his schooling as well and had just opened his own cross-fit training facility. Along with Roland, he is active in the sense that he enjoys his outdoor sports such as snowboarding, wake boarding, and slow pitch. Mike was more quiet than the other two but, in time, I could see Miranda was trying to dig deeper to see what there was below the surface of that quiet exterior.

Once we were completely done with our extended intros, Logan and Roland offered to set up a game of lawn darts which Amber and Demi agreed to join.

The sun slowly began to sink behind the trees and as it did, the air began to cool down. The hours had gone by unnoticed as everyone was laughing and having a great time. Lanterns were turned on and Logan brought out some glow sticks. Demi, Amber, Logan, and Roland all continued to play multiple lawn and drinking games; Demi had her sparking water, of course. I looked over as Miranda and Mike continued in deep conversation in which I had no clue what they were talking about, while Turner and I sat on the other side of the fire roasting marshmallows.

"Would you like a jacket or anything?" Turner offered as we sat having a casual conversation about simple things like our interests and hobbies, goals in life as well as what we do for work now. "I can grab you a sweater if you'd like and then maybe you would like to go for a walk?"

I looked over with a grateful smile. "Actually, I would appreciate a jacket. It's getting pretty chilly." I said as I rubbed my bare shoulders. "And a walk sounds wonderful."

Within minutes, I had a warm flannel jacket around my shoulders and he held my drink while helping me up.

"How does it look?" I ask as I pose with my hand on my hip and a smile on my face. "Does it go with my dress?"

"You look fantastic, and the colour brings out your eyes," He teased as he stared not only into my eyes but what felt was into my soul. Every time he did that I felt this weird connection between the two of us.

Just then Miranda looked up and asked, "Where are you two going?" Suddenly we aren't two alone; reality intrudes.

"What? Oh, um, just for a walk." I turned around and replied. "We shouldn't be too long. Is that alright, *Mom*?" I jokingly asked with a wink and a smile.

Miranda smiled back. "Oh, whatever. Have fun, but if you are gone too long I will come find you."

She then squinted at Turner and made a funny face before turning back where she continued to converse and laugh with Mike.

We left the group and headed along the road towards a hill that was used for tobogganing in the winter. For a few minutes, we walked in silence enjoying the evening while listening to the fires crackle and other campers talking and laughing in the surrounding sites.

"Sure is a gorgeous evening, don't you think?" Tuner offered as the first conversation starter. You can never go wrong with talking about the weather.

"Yes, it's perfect out. There's no wind, very few bugs, and the stars are starting to come out."

We both glance up, seeing the bright specks beginning to appear in the darkening sky.

"So, you mentioned earlier today that you were planning on moving?" He asked as we continued walking. "Do you mind if I ask where to?"

I placed my hands in my pockets before answering. "I'm moving to Toronto. I've got my place picked out and my first few months of rent pre-paid so this way I don't have to worry about not being able to find a job and not having spare cash for rent. I'm getting kind of nervous, actually."

"Oh?" He paused. "Why is that? Because it's so far away?"

"Well, no, not really. The distance doesn't bother me, it's more of the fact that I haven't told the others yet. I mean, Demi knows already, obviously, being my sister and all, but I haven't told Miranda and Amber that I will be leaving."

"Well, why haven't you told them yet? I mean they are your friends, right? What's the issue?"

I look over at him. Good Lord he is gorgeous. Okay, focus Dixie, he asked you a question. "The issue is that I really don't know how they are going to take it. It's…complicated. We may be close and have known each other since diapers but they aren't as open to spreading their wings as I am. They are content living this life here." We walk in silence for a brief moment. "But enough about me and my moving. What about you? I mean, what's your story? You said earlier by the fire that you are into landscaping and plan to start your own business with Logan. You love anything nature related, reading and enjoy Italian food. You have a cat named Gilbert and live with all three guys here with you. What else is there to know about you? Like, where are you from exactly? Somehow that was left out of our conversation earlier."

"Well," he said. "Believe it or not we are all from Toronto," he paused and I looked up stunned.

"Shut up." Did he seriously just say that? "Wait-wait-wait just a minute here. You are from Toronto?" I exclaimed as I tried to wrap my head around this new information before finally asking; "So, if you are from Toronto, what the heck are you doing all the way out here in Manitoba…of all the places in the world?"

He chuckled as we continued to walk. "Yeah, born and raised there, actually. The reason we come here is because I have relatives in Winnipeg. We used to come here every second summer but the past couple years, my grandmother has been sick and can't travel, resulting in us coming this way every year. For me it has gotten kind of boring just hanging out with relatives. So, now I bring the guys out camping while my parents and sister stay in the city."

I process this all for a moment. So, one, he lives *in* Toronto. The place I am about to move to. Not only that, but he has been coming *here* for *three* years and I have not met him until now? What the heck? Thanks, Cupid, for hooking a girl up. Either way, I'm just as dumbfounded.

"Well, that's really interesting," I say, flatly.

"Yeah, so maybe when you move we can grab a coffee or something? I can show you around the city a bit if you want."

I look over and cannot believe this is happening. "Um, yeah. I think I would like that. Thank you."

He smiled and rubbed the back of his neck. "You know, I've been here every summer for the past few years and this is the first time I've ever met someone who's caught my attention the way you have." He glanced at me as we reach the top of the hill.

"Excuse me?" We stop walking and I turn to face him. "I'm not sure I believe that."

"Why not? You are so different than anyone else I have ever met. You like the outdoors, you are a writer, you enjoy working with seniors and are genuine, not like majority of girls I've met before who put up a fake presence to impress a guy. I don't know, you're just... different, your energy is different. In a good way, though."

I blush again and look out at the view. The sun is almost fully set, the stars are shining extra bright tonight and the moon is full, watching every move the world makes.

"Well, that's really sweet of you to say," I look over at the silhouettes of the trees in the distance, "but I'm really nothing that special. I'm just a small-town girl with some dreams."

He then grabbed my chin and looked me in the eyes.

"You are so much more than that Dixie. I truly hope you believe that. And I want you to know that I think you will do great in Toronto. I haven't read your work but if it has your words and heart behind it, I'm sure it will catch a lot of people's attention."

I smiled once more. "Thank you. I've never had anyone say that to me before."

"Well, know it's true. I would really like to read what you have some time."

We stared at each other once more for a long moment and I began to bite my lip as my palms started to sweat. Turner slowly began to lean in. Holy cow, this isn't happening right now. This insanely attractive man is about to kiss me right now. I'm not sure I am ready for this. What if this is the last time I see him? Was he serious about showing me around? What if he is just saying all of this to get into my pants?

Just as he leaned in closer to kiss me I look down at the ground.

"I'm sorry." I whisper. "I'm just not ready for this. I mean, we just met and it's kind of soon."

He looked at me with both understanding and embarrassment in his eyes. "It's totally fine. I mean, I should be the one who's sorry. I don't know what I was thinking. I, um," he reached behind his head and turned away.

"Maybe we should just go back to the camp site?"

"Yeah, um…sure."

We walked back to the camp site in silence. *What is wrong with you Dixie? This could have been one of the greatest moments of your life and you turned it down. Way to go.*

Chapter Seven

As I imagined, the truth about my leaving erupted like a volcano. You would think that after knowing what I know so much about the laws of attraction, that I would learn how to control my life better. It's simple, ask, believe, receive, right? You ask for something in life whether it be good or bad; in my case I accidentally asked for this episode with Amber and Miranda to go badly because I repeatedly thought that it would go badly. Second, I believed that it would happen. I truly did believe it wouldn't go well, I even said it multiple times to Thelma, Demi, and Turner, what I now wished that I hadn't. Lastly, you receive what you ask for. Well, I got exactly as I asked for. After telling the girls my big news they decided to end our friendship pretty well right there.

"What do you mean you're moving to Toronto?" Miranda demanded. "When did you decide this? And you decide to tell us *now*? After we just planned the whole summer? I mean, come *on*, who does that?"

"Okay, there is no need to get upset like this. It's not like I'll never come home again, I'll be home every holiday and likely a few times in between," I urge.

"That is so not the point, Dixie. What ever happened to 'best friends for ever' and 'we will be there until the end', huh? I guess that is kinda shot now, isn't it? I seriously cannot believe you would do this to us and keep it a secret for so long. I thought we didn't keep secrets from each other."

"That's not fair. Why is it that whenever you all want to do something for yourselves, it's totally fine, but now that I want to, it's the end of the world? Like when Amber took a month last summer to go to Europe with her Aunt. I didn't complain, now did I? No, because that was a choice she made to better herself and, as the good friends we are, we understood. Only, now, I want to do something to better *myself* and you two are doing all that you can to make me feel bad."

Both Miranda and Amber stood there looking at me as though I was the worst person on Earth while Demi quietly stood off to the side when they then turned and locked their eyes on her.

"And, let me guess, you knew the entire time? Some friend you are, too, Dem," Amber scorned.

"Hey, now don't bring her into this, too. You guys can be upset with me all you want, but Demi has nothing to do with this." I pushed back. "This was my decision that I thought long and hard about. Yes, I understood that you would be upset, but as the good friends you claim to be, I honestly thought there was a slight chance that you would see where I am coming from on this. I mean, I don't want to spend the rest of my life here. I'm sorry that I want more out of life than working at the retirement home until it's my turn to move in. I, at least, need to know what else is out there. I need to know what my options are and I have to try to do something with my stories."

Miranda sneered. "You honestly think that someone is going to notice your work, Dixie?" She then crossed her arms and took a step towards me. "You are a small-town-country bumpkin with a few words that you put onto some paper. Congratulations. I mean, I wanted to be a doctor and it doesn't look like that is going to happen. I barely passed by bio final, my math sucks and I don't have good enough grades to make it into a decent university. I don't know where you are getting this inclination to become something so incredible, when that clearly won't happen. What, you think you have to be better than us at everything, Dix? Is that it? You know our biggest dreams won't come true so, you think that if you go out and try, you might actually pull it off and then come back to rub it in our faces?" She then stood there, glaring at me.

After a moment, I replied. "No, Miranda, that's not it at all. Do you remember back in grade two when our aunt passed away and she left us her books and movies? Well, I took what she and the books said to heart. I believe that if a person wants something bad enough, they will find a way to make it a reality, no matter how hard or easy it might be. You two may have given up on your dreams, but I haven't given up on mine. Now, I am going to Toronto whether you like it or not. I am going to get my books published and I am going to do something amazing with my life. All I ask is that you both stand by my side and try to see where I am coming from because you both know that I would be there for you."

Miranda, Amber, and Demi all stood there staring at me, before they responded.

"Come on, Amber, I think we are done. Clearly someone here needs more than what we and this town can give. You know, Dixie, we would have been happy for you and we would have understood, but the fact that you had to hide this for so long and then tell us practically at the last minute shows what you really think of us. I don't think there is any more point in trying. If we were your true friends like you said, you would have mentioned something sooner."

"But would you have understood? Honestly, Miranda, I don't think it would have mattered when I told you because you have one way of seeing things and clearly you only see this as my trying to find a way to hurt you guys, which is my very last intention. I didn't want to tell you because I knew you would be upset so I tried to find the best time to tell you-"

"There is no best time for something like this," Amber quietly said.

I looked at her with pain in my eyes.

"Exactly."

We all stood in silence once again until Miranda looked at Demi and then at me until I finally asked; "So, you're really going to walk away and end it like this?"

"No, Dix…you are. Come on, Amber," Miranda and Amber then turned and slowly walked away to Amber's car. Half way there Amber turned to look back with pain in her eyes, but then shook her head before continuing on. I stood watching them leave with my arms crossed, when Demi came and hugged me. I rested my head on her shoulder as a tear rolled down my cheek.

"It'll be okay," she said. "They will come around; it's just a shock to them right now. I promise, they will understand in a few days."

I continued to watch as they drove out of sight.

"Will they, though? I'm not sure about that this time."

The remainder of the summer passed without hearing much from Miranda and Amber. Our plans for camping on the weekends for the rest of the summer were all cancelled and we kept to ourselves. I must say that it hurt; after all these years, together, the secrets, the inside jokes, the lives we spent together were thrown out the window like that. All because I wanted more out of life. Was I wrong to want something else, to know what the world might hold for me? I sat back and thought about my Aunt Lisa's life. She worked as a banker for multiple years before throwing in the towel and risking everything. I remember Mom telling us how resentful my grandma was to her for packing up and leaving with only a few thousand dollars saved up, but once she began doing amazing things like getting her first commercial job, to eventually her own movie gigs and modeling roles, I knew my grandma couldn't have been more proud. The town, on the other hand, had it in for her. They began to think that she was too good to be around and she eventually lost all of her friends. Everyone would ignore her when she came back home. Was that what was going to happen to me? It looked like I'd already begun losing my friends. After some thought, I finally got it into my head that it would be worth it, and after everything I do and accomplish I will look back on all of this and be insanely proud of myself. Aunty Lisa would want me to do this.

For a few more weeks, Demi and I worked closely, with her following behind, learning all my tricks. Along with that, we visited Thelma every single day once our shifts were over.

"Well, dear, it's almost time, isn't it?" Thelma asked one evening after we clocked out. "You'll be packing up pretty soon, now won't you?"

"Actually, Thelma, I have everything already packed. All I have to do is load it into the U-Haul and drive out there. I'll be gone before you know it." I smiled and sipped a cup of tea.

"Well, I am proud of you, kid. You know, not everyone is as brave as you are to head off and attempt their dreams. If I know you, however, you will do incredible things and when you get those books published and onto the best seller lists, I'd better get a copy."

"You'll get one of the first ones printed."

"Hey, what about me?" Demi squeaked. "I better get one, too."

I laughed, "You both will and I'll sign each one specially for you guys."

"That's more like it," Demi beamed and got a bit more comfortable with her own cup of tea.

"Now, you have everything packed, apartment paid in advance, and everyone in town knows by now. Is there anything left for you to do?" Thelma asked as she checked her mental check list of my to do tasks.

"M-mm, I don't think so. I've already told the girls and we all know how that went so no, I think I have everything else already set."

"Well, good for you. You know I'm glad you didn't let your friends talk to you into staying here. One day they are going to look back on this and realize what a horrible mistake they made by throwing away this summer when you all could have been making memories together. Demi, Hun, have you heard from them much? Do they still talk to you at all?"

"Well," she said, crossing both legs on the couch. "They do talk to me here and there but not as much as they used to. They don't tell me things, like when we all used to hang out. But they did invite me to go camping with them a couple weeks ago. After talking with Dix, I went, but it was awkward. We met up with the same guys from before when we all went the first weekend but it wasn't much fun. They ended up clinging to the two guys; you remember Mike and Roland, right? And I hung out a bit with Logan but you could tell Turner felt left out. He kept asking about Dixie and where she was and all, but Miranda would tell him that you had more important obligations to attend to. So, I pulled him and Logan to the side at one point when the others were distracted and told them the truth. He said he would have to call you as soon as you move. So, I gave him your cell phone number. I hope that was okay?"

"Thanks Demi, I owe you one. It's totally fine. I really can't wait to move, Thelma. After all this crap that has gone down and how Miranda has turned so hard against me, I am now looking forward to getting out of here. I will miss you, Dem, everyone here and my family but I promise I won't miss this summer's drama."

"Well, you should look forward to going. That's the point in change. It means that something better is coming and that you have a lot to discover and look forward to. If there is anything I have learned from my time here on Earth it is that, one, you need to laugh often; two, you need to have fun and stay young for as long as you can; and, three, you need to travel.

"You must laugh because life is too short to be taken seriously. One day you will reach my age and ask yourself,

"Did I enjoy life the way it's meant to be enjoyed?" And trust me, you don't want to get to where I am, regretting not taking time to enjoy this short period you have. Now, you need to stay young as long as you can so that you *can* enjoy this time. Don't get caught up in working so hard that you forget how to live. Which leads to number three, travelling. You are starting now, by moving. You need to see what is out there. The world holds a lot of beauty that only a few people get to see, and it is a gift to us from the Creator, to be seen, walked upon, and touched. Now, if you live your life by those three rules, I promise that you will have one heck of a life to look back on and maybe, one day, to write about."

She winked and I took a moment to take her words all in.

"You know, you're right, Thelma. I do need to enjoy this, all of this from the move to my new adventure to everything. I hope that one day I can live half the life you have."

"And you will. Just keep your head up and don't let any negative people get into your head because the only reason they are such mood killers is because they believe that they cannot do what you are about to do. Your friend Miranda for example; she believes that she can't become what? A doctor you said, because she didn't get the grades. Well, if she wanted to become a doctor badly enough she would put in extra effort and retake the classes she needs and do everything and anything she can to make it happen, only she refuses because it's easier to say 'I can't,' rather than to try again. Too many people in this world are like that. It is easier to give up rather than to push and move the mountains that are in the way. But you two girls, I know it's in you to push, just like Lisa had it in her. I can see it in your eyes and I can feel it with your presence. Your energy is pulsing with determination and I know that you both will do incredible things with your lives, all you two must do is stick together. Demi, when you are finished school in a couple years and want to go to Toronto to live with Dixie, I know you will become more than a model. You, too, will become an inspiration to young girls everywhere, especially these small-town ones."

Demi sat up straight with hope and determination in her eyes. "Thank you, Thelma. That truly means a lot coming from you."

"Yes, thank you," I said. "Other than our parents and our grandma, you seem to be the only one to understand us fully."

"Do you know why?" she asked as she set her cup of tea on her coffee table. Demi and I both shook our heads. "Because I see me in both of you. The only way I lived the life I did was because of that determination. That constant striving for more. The belief that I could, and I don't want to see you two give up because it gets hard, or because someone befriends you. You both are worth so much more and I know that you can do anything you put your minds to. So, take care of yourselves, kids. Take care of each other and keep pushing one another until you reach a point where you have accomplished every goal you ever make, because the absolute best friends are the ones that understand what the other is going through and stay because they know it's worth it. So, don't sit and worry about Miranda and Amber, you will go out and meet a huge number of new people who will be ten times the friends that they ever were."

I took every single word Thelma spoke that day and locked it away in the back of my brain where it will stay forever. I wrote it down in a journal as well, because I believe she is right. I will want to look back on my life one day and pray that I will be so happy with the choices I've made, that it gets published into a book as well as, who knows, maybe even a movie. Only time will tell, I suppose.

Chapter Eight

Once boxes were packed into the U-Haul and every item was cleaned out of my room, I came downstairs to have lunch with my family before heading out. It would be a long road trip so my mom had packed me a couple coolers of food and a case of water to drink. I glanced at her face as we sat down to eat; I could see tears welling in her eyes.

"You do know that I will be back, right, Mom?" I tried to comfort her so she wouldn't fully break down.

"I know, it's just hard watching your baby girl leave the nest. I knew it would be hard but, no, never mind. I'm not going to cry," she wiped away a tear. "Who needs more lasagna?" She then began serving us each a piece even though we hadn't finished what was already on our plates. We then sat and had casual conversation about everyone else's plans for the remainder of the summer and beginning of fall. Mom was planning on working in her flower beds, trimming what was needed. Demi was obviously working, and Dad had work scheduled along with a fishing trip for a week with his buddies when he got back from dropping me off. Just as we finished up our meal, my grandmother walked in through the door.

"Oh, wonderful, I haven't missed you," she exclaimed and gave me a big hug after she walked around the table. "Are you all set and packed to go? I saw the U-Haul parked out front." She then handed me a gift bag. "I brought you some goodies for your new place."

I peeked inside the bag, unable to resist my curiosity. Inside was a clock, a few candles, one of her home-made pillows, and, pinned to the side, a Starbucks gift card. "Thank you Grandma. I can't wait to decorate my new place with all of this; it'll feel just like home."

"You're welcome, my dear," she began to play with

my hair, just as she had done when I was a little girl. "What time were you and your daddy planning on heading out?"

We all looked at the clock on the wall and realized it was already almost one o'clock. "Actually, Margaret, we were planning on being gone by one, so Dixie you better grab your bag, kiss your mother and we'll head out shortly."

My dad always hated being late.

"Yeah, good idea." We all cleared off the table and I picked up my last few belongings before heading out to the truck where I stood a moment before tears started rolling down my cheeks.

"Make sure you call me as soon as you get there. Also, call me tonight when you stop at the hotel and don't forget…"

"Mom, I got it. Everything will be fine; I will call you every night. Please stop worrying so much." I walked over and gave my mom the biggest hug imaginable. "I love you, but don't worry so much. I'm a big girl, I can do this."

She wiped a tear from my face.

"I know, it's just hard watching you go. I know you will be fine, but just promise me you will call or at least send me a text to let me know you're alive."

"Promise."

Next, was my Grandma's turn. Turning to her, I hugged her hard. "Thank you for everything, Grandma. I promise I'll call."

"That's what I wanted to hear, my dear. You be safe and don't talk to any funny looking strangers. Be careful of the good-looking ones, too, they can be just as sketchy. That's what you kids call it these days, isn't it?"

I laughed and agreed with her. "Yes, that's what some kids say. Okay, no talking to sketchy strangers and call you both as soon as I can. Got it. Dem? Your turn."

I pulled my little sister into my arms and neither of us wanted to let go.

"I'll miss you the most," I whispered. "Promise you will take care of yourself and keep your goals in mind. Don't let anyone bring you down to their level and remember that I will have a room ready for you whenever you want to come stay with me, got it? And if you can talk mom into letting you homeschool yourself let me know ASAP alright?" Demi cried and nodded. "Okay, now take care of Thelma for me, keep me posted with her at all times and I'll send her pictures in an email as soon as I can."

She looked me in the eyes with tears and mascara streaming down her cheeks.

"I love you, Dixie."

"I love you, too."

We both smiled watery smiles and I hopped into the truck while dad got it going. Before I knew it, we were off, and headed to my new home.

* * *

Three days of driving, two hotel stays, a bunch of gas stops and the odd fast food pit stop, and we finally made it to Toronto. As we entered the city I looked around at all the buildings full of businesses, full of people and full of opportunity, my heart beating so fast I could have sworn it was going to jump right out of my chest.

'This is it,' I thought to myself. 'I finally made it.' I smiled as Dad punched our destination into the GPS while he asked to keep my eyes out for crazy drivers.

"This city is a busy one, Dixie. Very fast paced and full of energy, I hope you are ready for this," he gripped the steering wheel tight and checked the GPS for directions.

"You all really do need to stop worrying about me so much. I am more than capable of getting around and taking care of myself, I need you all to trust me, it's not like I'm thirteen. I'm graduated, eighteen and now classed as an adult. You all need to relax a bit." I mention as I continue to stare out the window at all the tall buildings that we passed by.

He then looked at me with a smile on his face, "I know you can, Hun, but you're our baby girl and always will be, so we can't help but worry every now and again. I know you will make us proud out here, there is so much to learn and see and do, not like at home. You can only go up from here and when you do, we will all be even more proud than we already are."

"Thanks, Dad. That really means a lot," I smiled and we drove on weaving our way in and out of traffic.

It took us an hour and a half longer to find my new place because Dad took a wrong turn thirty minutes in. Upon arriving, we met the building manager, received my keys and headed up to my new home. Once inside I looked around at the tiny, open space. It was a small one bedroom, one bath with a very tiny kitchen that connected to the living area. It was cute and I had a feeling that I was going to love it, once I made it my own.

"Well, what do you think, Hun? It doesn't seem too bad, a bit smaller than you're used to, but how much space does one small person need, right?" He rubbed my shoulder.

"I like it a lot, Dad. Thank you again for helping with the first few months' rent. I will be handing out resumes as soon as I get settled in."

"No problem, you'll be on your feet in no time. However, if you ever need any more help, you make sure to call us and I will transfer you money into your account, alright?"

I smiled, "Thanks, Dad."

"Now, how about we bring your stuff in and set up so I can get going. I don't want to miss my flight home. If I do, I will be rooming with you."

"Ew, yeah we don't want that. You snore too loud."

We both chuckled and headed back down to the truck

where we spent the next two hours bringing in my things and setting up. Once we were finished and we said our 'good byes' my dad headed off and left me in my new home, perhaps for years.

The first night was eerie. The traffic was heavier than I'm used to out on the farm and I could hear people talking as they walked past my door to get to their own apartments. I lay awake the majority of the night listening to the sound of everything going on, not to mention the rain storm that decided to settle in around two in the morning. The lightning flickered in my windows and the wind howled as it weaved in and out of the tall buildings. I think that once I can figure my way around here and find out where my place is in this town it'll be alright, but until then I'm going to hide under my blanket until I get enough sleep.

The next morning, I awoke around ten o'clock to the sun shining, rain drops on my window and a pigeon sitting on my window sill. I then slowly rolled out of bed and dodged a bunch of my unpacked boxes to get to the bathroom where I would shower, tame my hair, and get dressed into my favorite pair of jeans and pink hoodie that I collected at a camp in Rock Ridge Canyon a few years back.

Once ready to face the day, I decided to call my parents and Demi to let them know that I survived the first night.

"Dixie!" Demi squealed through the phone line. "How are you? It's so late! I wasn't sure if you were alive. Did you sleep in or what?"

"Hey Dem. Yeah, I slept in. I didn't get much sleep at all last night. The traffic was way busier than back home and the thunder storm was pretty loud last night. I don't even know when I fell asleep but I know it was late. Did Dad make it home okay?"

"Yes, he did. Mom drove to Winnipeg to pick him up

last night. They ran to town to go help someone with something this morning, I can't remember, but they said that if you call, you are supposed to look in the front zipper of your suit case. They apparently left something for you in there."

"Oh?" I said curiously as I walked to my bedroom to dig though my suitcase. "What is it?" I asked as I opened the front zipper.

Inside was a white envelope and inside that, was five hundred dollars as well as a note that read "*Go buy yourself something nice. Love you lots. Love: Mom and Dad.*"

"I'm not sure, did you find it?"

"I did, it's some money. Make sure to tell them thanks for me. I'll have to call them again tonight."

"Oh nice! And okay, will do. So, what's the plan today?"

"I'm not sure, maybe head out and start discovering this place once I find my coffee pot. We unpacked most of my stuff but there's still a few things left to dig out apparently."

"Oh, well that sounds fun. Make sure to take some pictures while you're out and about then and send them to me later so I know that you aren't living in some scummy part of town. And, like Grandma said, don't talk to anyone sketchy. Trust no one. Got it?"

I laughed. "Got it. I'll text you later this afternoon okay? I better get going, I can't afford crazy phone bills!"

"Sounds good. I love you, Dixie."

"I love you, too, Dem. Have a good day and tell Mom and Grandma that I'll call them tonight."

"Deal."

We both hung up the phone as I sat on the edge of my bed, looking around my new place.

"Well, let's see what this world has to offer," I said to myself, getting up from my bed, and tucking the envelope of money away into my purse.

Once down the stairs and out the front door to my

apartment building I looked both ways to see what nearest restaurant or café I could find and to my surprise I couldn't see any form of either. So, my gut instinct was to hail a cab and ask the driver the best place to go.

I wound up at a small coffee shop after a ten-minute drive. I'm not sure what to expect but I assume it'll be a lot like Tim Horton's. I hope it is anyway, the cab driver said its where a lot of people on the go get their morning coffee. Whether that's true or not, I guess I will find out. I went in, ordered a coffee and a light breakfast and sat down to eat. I can honestly say that this has to be the most uncomfortable I have ever felt. By the looks of everyone else, I am going to have to invest in a new wardrobe, everyone dresses so modishly, I can't help but feel like a grub. Maybe I was wrong, maybe this was a bad idea moving here. I mean, I don't know a soul, I have no idea where or what everything is and I am literally a nobody here. Not one person has made eye contact with me since arriving. I hope Thelma was right, that this will all be worth it in the end.

After finishing half of my coffee and my meal, I decided to go back to my apartment, do some writing and create a new vision board to help me focus and create my new life. At least that way I will get something done. Maybe later I will even whip out a map and try to figure out where to go from here.

Chapter Nine

The next few weeks trickled by as I found my way around the crazy new world I lived in. Each day I made a point to try and discover a new area and the wonders it had to hold. Out of all the places I've discovered so far, I must say that Yorkville is my most favorite place to wander. It's an amazing shopping area that I find myself wandering for hours causally window shopping, almost every weekend. I've never seen such beautiful clothing, hand bags, jewelry and so much more. It's a place where I find I can relax, take in the expensive taste of the city and envision my future years in this place.

I will normally start my days with a simple coffee indoors, people watching, before I make my way from shop to shop, letting my thoughts and plans for my life take over.

A few other places that I've discovered is a great movie theatre at Yonge and Eglinton, which across from it holds a Keg restaurant, Starbucks and a few small restaurants.

I get my groceries from fruit sellers, butcher shops, and supermarkets rather than a small grocery store like we have back home. It's nice to have options of where and what to buy when it comes to my meals. Over the course of the past weeks I've even managed to start remembering some of the market owner's names.

Gina is my favorite. She is a tiny, middle aged Korean woman who sells fruit and flowers within the market. In time, we have stopped and spoken and gotten to know one another. She lives with her husband in a small town-house just down the road. She has two children, one boy who is eighteen and a girl who is seventeen, both finishing up school within the next year or two, and headed off to university. Gina runs her stand to help pay for her children's future education. Once I told her my dreams and wishes and the reason I have moved here, Gina became generous and understanding of my own situation. Now, every Saturday that I head down to restock my kitchen, Gina gifts me one of her flowers along with my fruit purchase from her. It's a small gesture that has meant the world to me. I haven't gotten to know anyone yet, so I'll take any form of outside communication and relationship that I can. Even if it means chatting it up with my local market owners.

Other than shopping and wandering the city, I managed to find a job at a small café not too far from my apartment. I have been lucky to work mostly Monday to Friday and the odd Saturday, eight o'clock to open to four o'clock before shift change. It's not my ideal job, but hey, these bills won't pay themselves.

In all, I found myself falling more and more in love with the city the longer I was there. It didn't take long before I was able to comfortably call Toronto 'home'. I did, however, miss my family and Thelma, but that's where phone calls, and writing letters to Thelma, came in handy. Once a week I would write a letter to Thelma, along with sending some pictures of what I was up to that week. In return, I would receive words of hope and inspiration to keep on going with what I was doing with my life. It helped to reassure me that my heart was right when it told me I was on the right path in life.

One sunny afternoon, while I sat in my apartment working on a book project, I received a phone call from an unknown, Toronto number. Curious, I answered.

"Hello?" I said as I placed my laptop beside me on the couch.

"Hey. Dixie?" A man's voice replied on the other end.

"Yes?"

"Oh, great. Um, this is Turner, from the park this

summer."

I sat in silence for a brief moment. Is this really him? I hadn't heard from him since seeing him earlier this summer. I couldn't believe it.

"Oh!" I finally replied. "Hey, how are you?"

"I'm good. Sorry it took me so long to give you a call. Demi mentioned that you made it to Toronto safely a while ago. I thought I'd let you settle in before giving you a call."

"Oh, well thank you. That's very considerate."

"So, how are you liking the city so far?"

"It's wonderful," I told him. "There is so much to see and do compared to back home. The few people I've met all seem so nice. It's definitely something else."

"That's great. You managed to find your way around alright then?"

"Slowly. I'm new to the whole transit and subway idea but I'm catching on. I'm used to driving myself around but here, I'm not even going to attempt it. Not yet anyway." I laughed. "So, how about you? How have you been?" I asked.

"Oh, you know. I've been alright. The guys and myself came home early this year from camping and we got a head start on work, picking up a few landscaping jobs here and there to get our name out. I've been thinking of you a lot these past few months. Demi told Logan and I what happened, so I was bummed out not to see you anymore." He paused.

"Well, aren't you sweet," I smiled.

"I do what I can. So, um, seeing as you are here and all settled in, I was wondering if you would be interested in maybe trying something new? I have tickets to a Blue Jays game this weekend and thought you might want to check it out with me?"

I took his request in and thought about it. "Like, on a date?" I finally asked. Was Turner, Mr. Gorgeous from the park, who I have thought of constantly, asking me out on a date?

"Yeah... like a date. That is, if you are up for that."

I thought about it again. "I would like that. Thank you." I smiled and leaned back into the couch as I pulled my knees up and began to play with my hair.

"Awesome. So, it will start around two o'clock. I can pick you up earlier if you'd like. Maybe we can grab some lunch beforehand?"

"Sure. I have the day off so any time works for me." I nibbled my lower lip.

"Okay. How about I pick you up around twelve?"

"Sure! I'm just off Queen," I quickly gave him the address of my building. "If you message me when you get here, I'll meet you outside."

"Sounds great. So, I will see you Saturday then. Twelve o'clock."

"It's a date." I replied clearly excited.

"It's a date. Well, I better get back to work. Logan's giving me a dirty look for making him do the heavy lifting by himself," he chuckled.

"Sounds good. Say hi to Logan for me and I will see you Saturday."

"Will do. Bye." He hung up the phone before I did.

I sat in silence for a while smiling to myself unable to believe that Turner actually called me and asked me out on a date. My heart was fluttering.

* * *

The rest of the week flew by as the anticipation of our date grew stronger each day that came and went. On Saturday morning I woke to a phone call from Demi, asking about my week and what was planned for the day. After telling her about my upcoming date and how my week at work went, she told me how school was going and how Miranda and Amber both avoid her like the plague. She also mentioned that Thelma had been in and out of the hospital but overall was doing well.

Once our conversation was over I got up from my bed and headed for a shower before blow-drying and then curling my hair. Once my beachy curls were perfect, I made myself a cup of coffee, sat down in the living room on the couch and enjoyed the sunlight shining through the pale blue curtains. The calmness within my apartment was peaceful. There I sat for the next hour, sipping my coffee and casually scrolling the internet for book publishers and agents to represent me and my work.

After jotting down a few new phone numbers and email addresses, I decided to get up and apply some make up before my date with Turner. It was only nine o'clock by this point so I researched how to contour my face and figured I would give it a try to take up some time before I had to run to the market to get my upcoming weeks' worth of groceries.

Come lunch time, my phone rang and it was Turner. He told me that he would be at my place in about fifteen minutes. So, in that time, I grabbed my purse before slipping on my flip flops and made my way down two flights of stairs and out the front door where I waited for Turner.

He pulled up in a cab and hopped out to welcome me with a hug and held the door as I climbed inside the cab. Once we were inside, Turner gave the driver a new location and we were on our way.

"You look stunning," Turner said with a smile as he fastened his seat belt.

"Thank you. As do you." I replied.

"Thanks. So, how was your week?"

"Oh, you know. Busy with work and writing, but over all pretty decent. How was yours?"

"Same, minus the writing," he smiled again. Lord, I almost forgot how gorgeous his smile was. "Logan and I have been getting more calls lately to fix up people's yards

80

and such so it's been great. Where are you working?"

I placed my purse beside us on the seat. "I found a job at a café not too far from here actually. It's nothing big or exciting, but it'll definitely do for now."

"Oh, a café. That's nice. There's nothing wrong with food."

It was my turn to smile this time.

"Speaking of food. I know of this great restaurant called "Hole in the Wall". It's a Greek restaurant. I think you will love it.

"Greek food? Sounds delicious!"

We spent the rest of the twenty-minute ride catching up from the summer as well as discussing what actually happened between myself, Amber and Miranda.

Once inside the restaurant, Turner held a chair out for me before seating himself. As he sat down a waiter poured us some water and told us that he would be back shortly to take our orders.

"So, what sort of things do you like to eat?" I asked, looking at the menu.

"Normally I am a burger or steak kind of guy. I try to eat semi healthy but that doesn't always work out." I sipped some water. "I like the chicken souvlaki here though. They are usually pretty good, but so is moussaka or the traditional Greek salad... I don't sound very manly ordering a salad, do I?" He smirked.

"Well, not overly," I laughed back. "But the salad does sound delicious. I think I'll have that."

"Good choice. I'm going to do the moussaka because I know it's great and I won't look so girly."

The waiter had come and taken our order, while we sat and discussed our plans for the upcoming fall and winter. I had told him my plans weren't changing a whole lot, I would continue to work on my writing as well as finding an agent, along with work at the café. I didn't have a whole lot planned at all. Turner on the other hand, had been picking up as many jobs as he could before the winter and had been going back to school for another year to finish up his trade for his journeyman's license.

The hour passed as we finished our meals, laughed and thoroughly enjoyed one another's company. Once we were done and Turner paid for our lunch, hailed us another cab and we were then off to the baseball game at the Rogers Center.

I had never been to a real baseball game before, so I had no idea what to expect. When we got inside to find our seats, the energy was overwhelming. The stands were already three quarters full as we found our way up multiple flights of stairs and across handfuls of people and seats to find our own place to sit. We sat down and in front of us was the biggest ball diamond I had ever seen in my life. There were lights, and nets and players warming up on the field. This was definitely something new and I couldn't have been more excited to share that experience with Turner.

The game eventually started and the crowds' energy became stronger. I however, knew very little about the sport itself but it didn't take long for me to get the jist of it. Turner and I spent the next few hours cheering and screaming for our team while snacking on peanuts and sipping bottles of water in between innings.

Over all, the date had been a lot of fun and full of new experiences. We arrived back at my place around supper time so I offered to cook us both something after a day of Turner treating me. After agreeing, we made our way up to my apartment where I started cooking some rosemary chicken thighs and baked vegetables as Turner watched me while sitting on the opposite side of the counter on a bar stool. I didn't have a lot in my fridge but that morning's grocery run left me with enough food to make a decent meal.

"This is delicious," Turner commented as we sat in a

corner at a tiny table just off the kitchen. "Where did you learn to cook like this?" He asked.

"Well, my parents are both relatively old fashioned and believe that people should learn how to cook at a young age, so I started making meals around the time I was fourteen, plus I picked up a few pointers while working at the retirement home. The cooks there taught me a lot." I smiled as I ate.

"Well, it's very impressive. I won't lie when I say I don't know how to cook anything like this. I can do your basic mac and cheese and some hot dogs but that's all... aside from barbequing."

"Well, you're in luck then, now aren't you?" I said as I was about to take another bite of my meal.

He stared at me with those baby blue eyes. He had the same sparkle in them as he did when we first met. "Indeed I am."

We stared at each other for a few seconds before I felt myself begin to blush. I put my head down as I bit my lip and quickly took another bite and stared around the room. Looking anywhere other than his into his eyes.

That made Turner chuckle. "So, how is your sister doing these days? Logan mentioned that they had been talking off and on."

I looked back at him, the redness in my face fading away. "Oh, she's good. I talked to her this morning, actually. She's been busy with work, school, and volleyball mostly."

"That's good. Do you plan on going back to see your family any time soon?"

"Mm, I don't think so. I do miss them a lot, but I haven't had my job for very long and can't imagine getting much time off any time soon so I'll likely wait until closer to Christmas before heading back."

"Makes sense. I bet it's difficult being away in a new city with new people and a whole new way of living compared to what you are likely used to."

"Yeah, some days it's tough and I miss home, but then I remember why I'm here and it helps. If all else fails, I call my family and it makes me feel a bit better. Demi had mentioned a few times, taking the rest of her schooling by correspondence and moving here with me but I'm not sure our parents will go for it. I mean, it would be great if they did because she could move in with me and we could split the rent and such but it's a long shot for them to agree. Especially with her being as young as she is."

"Well, I'm sure it will work out how its suppose to. I know Logan would be pretty excited if she moved here."

"Oh, I'm sure he would too," we both smiled once more.

"Well, cheers to new beginnings," Turner raised his glass of water. "You are a strong woman for moving out here on your own to chase your dreams. I'm glad I got the chance to get to know you better."

I raised my own glass and clinked it with his.

"Cheers to new beginnings," I said. "And thank you for calling me. I had a great day, so thank you."

"Pleasure's all mine," he winked.

We finished up our meal and tidied the dishes before settling in on the couch to watch some T.V and visit some more for an hour before he had to go.

Once he was ready to leave, Tuner stood at the doorway. "Well, thank you for a great day," he said. "I'm glad that you agreed to give me a chance even though it took me so long to call you."

"It's not a problem," I replied, arms casually crossed, hugging myself. "It was nice to get out and do something different aside from working and writing or watching T.V."

"I'm glad." Turner paused. "So, if it's alright with you, I would like to see you again."

I looked up into his eyes once again and found myself unable to say no. Not that I wanted to say no anyway.

"Yeah, I'd like that," I said.

Turner smiled. "Me, too," he then reached out and began to play with my curls that we're clearly coming lose.

My heart began to race and I started to bite my lower lip again.

"I love it when you do that," he said softly.

"Do what?" I asked as I tilted my head in confusion and bit my lip some more.

"That," he then gently grabbed my face, pulled me in and kissed me.

It felt as though time had stopped as my heart raced harder and I became dizzy. I grabbed his waist as he pulled away from our kiss and apologized.

"I'm sorry. I've just been wanting to do that since the summer."

I looked up and stared deep into his eyes, "Don't apologize," I said with a smirk, before

pulling him in and kissing him again.

I don't know what it is about this guy, but I look forward to figuring it out.

Chapter Ten

It was a brisk Tuesday autumn afternoon when I found myself in a corner of a local Starbucks, sipping a white chocolate mocha and working on my next novel when a young girl in her early to mid-twenties walked through the door and made eye contact with me as I glanced up. She smiled a warm smile and continued to the till to place her order. I turn to look around and take in the atmosphere. The warmth of the fireplace, the smell of the coffee and tea along with the quiet chit chat of the small hand full of others sitting around, enjoying the afternoon.

"Nice day, isn't it?" Someone suddenly asked from beside me. It's the girl I made eye contact with. She's fairly tall, just under six feet I would guess. She had blonde hair all tied up in a messy bun atop her head and is wearing a long grey knit sweater, leggings and a maroon scarf and brown knee high boots. Her face had a warm complexion and a pair of hipster looking glasses atop her nose. Along with that she had the longest eyelashes I've ever seen on someone in my life.

'Those can't be real,' I thought to myself. Just below the outer corner of her eye, she had a beauty mark. I just sit and stare at her. "I mean, it's not too cold out for this time of year. My name's Naomi. Do you mind if I sit with you?" Seriously, who is this pretty? I'm slightly jealous.

"Oh, yeah. Um…sure," I say to her. I'm surprised that someone is talking to me. I moved to Toronto at the end of summer and honestly haven't made any friends yet. Well, I have hung out with Turner a couple of times, but that is about it for where friendships are sitting. I have been so absorbed into finding a publisher and writing new stories that I neglected to put effort into making any other actual friends. I guess when your so-called 'best friends' turn on you, you tend to put a bit of a wall up.

"Thanks," she smiled again. "This is my favorite place to come on days like today. It's so warm and inviting, don't you think?"

I look around briefly. "Yes, this is one of my favorite places to come, too. I'd never been to a Starbucks until I moved out here a couple months ago and I have to say that I really enjoy it."

"I couldn't agree more. What are you drinking? I have a dark cherry mocha coming, it's my favorite. I usually only find it in the winter time but occasionally one of the workers make it for me if I sweet talk him enough."

Seriously, there is something about her that is drawing me in. I can't help but like her. I smile awkwardly once I realize how creepy I'm being by staring so much. I quickly look at my drink on the table. "I got the white chocolate mocha. It's not too bad, a little stronger tasting than I'm used to."

Naomi smirked, "I know, right? I find it's what gives the drinks their flavor though. The teas aren't too bad either. Oh! And the food here. To die for!" She then looked at my lap top and note pad sitting on the table in front of me. "What are you working on?" She questioned.

I look down at my pile. "Oh, it's nothing." I paused and she looked at me blankly. "Okay, it's not nothing. It's a novel that I'm working on. I'm trying to become a published author. It's kind of a dream I've had since I've was a little girl." Without warning, I have a sudden flashback to when Miranda, Amber, Demi, and I first began vision boards together.

"That's really interesting. What are you writing about? Is this your first book?"

"Naomi!" One of the baristas yell from behind the till.

"Hold that thought," Naomi got up and scurried off to grab her drink. She quickly returned sipping her mocha and sat down beside me once again. "Sorry about that. If you don't grab your order right away the baristas tend to get a bit annoyed. But anyway, what is it that you are writing about?"

"It's okay," I reply. "I'm actually writing about a young girl trying to make her way in a world filled with close minded people. She has a dream to make it big but no one believes in her. So, one day she decides that she has had enough of everyone's attitude and moves to a big city to live out her dream. In the end, she does more than she ever thought possible and blows everyone's mind. It's kind of based on a true story of this girl I know." I again flash back to my younger years. "And, um…no, this isn't my first book, I've written a couple already. Only, I'm still not sure what my next steps will be. Well, no, I shouldn't say that. I know that I have to find an agent before I can find a publisher, my problem is that I don't know where to find one. I've been looking in newspapers and online but no one will take the time to read my work. Half of the people I've called won't even respond to my message. Like, I knew that this wouldn't be the easiest thing in the world to do, publish a book I mean, let alone a best seller, but I thought someone would be interested by now. It's been three months of non-stop searching with no luck. I know in my heart there is someone out there who is waiting for a story like mine to make big. My only problem is finding them."

Naomi stared at me, with pity in her eyes.

"I'm sorry, that was a lot to dump and well, I just met you. Um…" I trailed off.

"No, no don't worry about it. I'm glad to listen. You clearly are having a hard time and I get it. Toronto can be tough. Nobody takes extra time to do anything around here. Everything is rush, rush, rush. Rush to go to work. Rush there to run some errands. Rush to meet friends and then rush though the visit to get somewhere else. What ever happened to enjoying the simple things in life and taking time to help others is beyond me…If I were an agent, I'd at least consider what you have to offer."

"Thanks," I said in reply.

Naomi then stared out the window in front of us. There were people walking by in every direction. You could feel the buzz of the city even in doors. "Do you want to go for a walk? I mean, unless you have somewhere else you have to be."

After living in this city alone for the past few months, I wasn't about to turn down a possible friend. "I don't have anywhere I need to be, I'll come with you." I packed up my computer and the rest of my belongings, grabbed my jacket and coffee and we both left the building, into the crisp, fresh air.

We spent the next three hours wandering the streets simply talking about our lives, goals and biggest dreams. We discussed our pasts and where we came from. Even though Naomi looked like your average city girl, I found out that she was raised by a single mother who worked three jobs just to keep food on the table and a roof over her head. She was an only child who longed to have a father figure like so many other girls have had the privilege of growing up with, much like myself.

She told me that he left the day she was born because she was born a girl. He apparently wanted a son and once that didn't happen and he found out couldn't ever happen with his wife of two years, due to the fact that there were complications with the birth, leaving Naomi's mother unable to conceive again. He packed his things, left and was never heard from again. She said that people think he is in Vancouver but no one is sure. So, throughout her entire life growing up with only her mother, Naomi always swore that one day she would become something big so that she could help her mother retire early as kind of a repayment for holding on through the toughest part of both of their lives. She said it was a struggle. She never really had friends growing up either and was a bit of an outcast in school, but now that she was out and about working to help pay the bills, she was slowly but surely finding herself.

And I thought a simple argument with my friends was tough. After talking to Naomi, it made me realize just how blessed I am in life. I have a family that loves me, I have work friends from back home that enjoy my company, I have a roof over my head that my parents are mostly paying for and I don't have to worry where my next meal is coming from. A lot of people forget about those little things and they focus solely on material things, believing that this is what makes a person happy, when your happiness can only be created by yourself. If you chose to be happy with what you have in life, then you have it made. If you feel as though material objects are the only thing that can bring you joy, then I feel terribly sorry for those people because "stuff" can come and go. That new handbag you just bought? You might like it now, but what happens when you get bored of it in a couple months? Or that new car that your daddy just bought you? What if you write it off? That's when a person becomes sad or depressed and needs more. Those who are happy to have even a bike to ride or simply a healthy set of legs, they are the ones that are set and will have a much more fulfilled life than those who cannot see the beauty in the simpler things.

After another hour of walking and discussing our lives, Naomi turned to face me excitedly. "I think I know someone!" she exclaimed.

"Beg your pardon?" I asked.

"I think I know someone who might read your story. That is, if she isn't too busy." She smiled again. "Oh, my gosh, why didn't I think of her before?"

"What? Who?"

"Well, there is this friend I have who I happened to do a huge favor for a few months back and he said that if I ever need a favor in return to give him a call. Well, anyhow, he has an aunt who is head of some big publishing company. If I get hold of him maybe he could get your book to her. It's a totally genius plan. Do you have any copies laying around at home?"

"Well, I do but you don't need to do that. Use your favour on me, I mean. I'm sure I can find a publisher and agent, don't worry."

Naomi stared at me blank faced. "No, we are going to use it. We must, how else are you going to get your work in? You said yourself that no one will give you the time of day. Well, if this lady gets something from her nephew surely she will at least *read* it. What do you say?"

I thought about it for a moment and then finally agreed to do so. What do I have to lose? Here I have someone trying to help me and even be a decent friend to me, the least I can do is give it a shot. "Okay, we will do it. Thank you so much for this." Right then was when my phone started to ring. It was Demi.

"Hello?" I answered.

"Hey, Dix, are you busy?" her voice was shaky.

"No, why? What's up? Is something wrong?" Naomi looked at me, worried.

"Um, it's Thelma. She…um."

"Demi…What happened?" I knew right away what she was going to say and my heart begun to sink into the pit of my stomach.

"Thelma passed away this morning. I'm not one hundred percent sure what happened, but part of it had to do with her liver. I know she's been sick off and on for a while, but no one made a big deal out of it until lately. I told you the other day she was in the hospital. Well, Andrea called me today and told me the news. Her funeral will be Friday. I know it's already Tuesday but do you think you can make it home? I don't want to go by myself."

I am in utter shock and could not believe that this was happening.

"Um, yeah." I paused. "I'll catch a flight either tomorrow night or by Thursday for sure. I'll let you know and talk to you then, okay?"

"Okay. Text me when you know what time you'll be in Winnipeg? I'll come pick you up."

"Deal," I hung up the phone and explained to Naomi what had just happened, as I wiped a tear from my cheek. We both stood there in shock.

"I'm really sorry to hear that, Dixie. If it makes it any better, I can try to get your story in while you're away. This way, maybe when you get back you will have some good news."

"I would honestly appreciate that. Would you like to come over tomorrow by chance? I can have it ready by then. I work until four o'clock but I will be free in the evening. I should start packing I suppose.

"Yeah, I would love that. I will bring us something to eat and I can help you pack. I have this whole week of so I don't have plans for much of anything."

"It's a date then." I looked at my watch. "Well, I should get going, it's a bit later than I thought. I will get my manuscript up and ready for you. Do you have a phone? I can give you my number and address?"

"Oh yeah, for sure," Naomi reached into her pocket and handed me her phone. I added my number into her contacts. "Alright, I will see you tomorrow then. It was nice meeting you, Dixie."

"You, too. Thank you for the afternoon. It was great to finally meet someone who is willing to give me the time of day. I better run though. See you."

We both turned our separate ways when I heard her on her phone the second we parted. "Hey, Josh, how are you? Oh, good, I'm good as well, thank you. Hey, remember a while ago you said that if I ever need anything, to give you a call? Well, I have a *huge* favor to ask of you…"

Chapter Eleven

Naomi came over the next day just had she had promised she would. She knocked on my door with take-out bags of Chinese food in hand, and just as I opened the door, she flooded in and set the bags on the counter.

"I have great news," she said, not even waiting for a greeting. "So, I talked to my friend yesterday and told him we needed some help and he agreed to ask his aunt if she could take a peek at it!"

"What? Are you serious? Oh, my goodness! That's fantastic. Thank you so much!"

My eyes were, I'm sure, as round as dinner plates. I could not believe he had agreed to help us, to help me, even though he had no idea who I was.

"Yeah, and I have even better news," she paused and smiled widely.

"What? What is it?" I demanded, confused.

"He called me back late last night and said that his aunt agreed to read it! Isn't that wonderful?"

My mouth dropped open. Had this seriously just happened? I had been searching for weeks with zero luck and, with just one phone call, I now had someone willing to look at my work?

"I can't believe this is happening, I owe you big time, Naomi. Especially if this goes through."

"Don't worry about it, Dixie. It's the least I could do to welcome someone into the city."

I grabbed a folder from my night stand and handed it to her, feeling almost nervous.

"This is it, all three hundred and twenty-eight pages of it. I wrote my email and contact number on the top just in case," I said, pretending my hand wasn't shaking.

"Holy cow, that's wonderful. Can I read a part of it?"

"Of course," I said, motioning to the couch. "I have to finish packing, but make yourself at home. Did you want something to drink?"

"No, I'm good," Naomi didn't waste any time opening the folder and diving into the first page as I made my way to my small, very small, closet to continue putting together everything I might need for a weekend.

The rest of the evening passed peacefully as we talked, packed, and ate our General Tso's chicken and fried rice. Naomi and I got to know each other a bit better, as we talked about ourselves, Thelma, old friends and again, the lives we wanted. It turned out that we have a lot more in common than I thought we did. We both planned on becoming something great; Naomi dreams of becoming a realtor and owning a home of her own and getting out of her tiny, expensive rental. We both love the idea of traveling and dream of finding our own Mr. Wonderful, wherever he may be. I have a feeling that this newly formed friendship will be long and lasting.

* * *

The second I reached the arrivals area of the airport I found Demi running at me with arms wide open.

"Dixie!" she squealed and jumped into my extended arms.

"Hey Dem, I've missed you so much," I say, hugging her tightly. "How are you?"

"As good as one can be, under the circumstances. I mean, with Thelma and school and the girls and work and…"

"Whoa, settle down, what do you mean the girls? What's going on?"

"Oh, it's nothing, never mind. How are you with everything?"

"No, Dem tell me!" I insist, instinctively feeling something is not right. "What's wrong?"

"Nothing's wrong. Just… don't bother talking to them while you're here. They've changed since you've left.

And not in a way that would benefit you in any way, shape or form." She paused as she took note of the look on my face, which must have shown exactly how I felt.

"They're just jealous, Dixie, it's fine. We have more important things to worry about, such as the funeral. Let's focus on that, okay? Now hurry up, get in the car and let's go get some take out for the ride home. I'm starving."

With that we headed out into the brisk autumn air, and piled into Demi's silver, slightly rusted Sunfire.

On the way home, we talked about the past few months. It turns out that Miranda and Amber seem to have developed a great dislike for me since I left.

I can hardly believe the things that Demi tells me. Things I never would have thought my two life-long friends capable of. Who were these people? How could they believe such things of me, much less repeat them? I left town because no one wanted to know me? I couldn't get a date? I had to create an entirely new life where no one knew me because I wasn't capable of success at home?

So much for friendship. I had known that they were upset, but I had thought that they would be happy for me, eventually. Making up false rumours, hurtful rumours... this was a side of them that I had never suspected existed, and it hurt.

And the things that they were saying about Turner and the others was equally perplexing. Their claims of Toronto boyfriends who would be coming to visit at Christmas was confusing, to say the least, given what I knew from Turner.

I was quickly concluding that I had no idea who my two best friends for the past fifteen years were.

Seeing my hurt and confusion, Demi wisely changed the subject, instead addressing something that she had briefly brought up with me through phone calls and messages, but with much more seriousness than I expected from my high-spirited little sister.

"So, what do you think about my moving to Toronto?"

"What?" I mentally give my head a shake; weren't we

just talking about Miranda and Amber and their rather extreme reaction to my moving?

"Dixie, it's not like I haven't mentioned this before."

"Well, yeah, I get that, but I thought you were going to wait until after you graduated. Do you honestly think that Mom and Dad will let you before you're done school?" I question.

Demi has mentioned occasionally wanting to move to Toronto with me, only she didn't know what to do about school. She had one year left, but was eager to get out and start her modeling career and where to better start than my new home town?

"Yeah, so after begging Mom and Dad, along with explaining to them the benefits of home educating myself, I think I am slowly wearing them down. Like, I can come live with you, get a part time job to help pay the bills, school myself in your apartment and then in my spare time I can head out, find myself the odd modeling gig here and there until I get my name out about. They're willing to give me the year. I know it seems like a farfetched dream but I think I can do it. What do you think?" Demi glanced at me hopefully, sipping her bottle of water whilst driving down the highway.

"I will talk to Mom tomorrow," I sigh, looking at her hopeful expression and wondering how I got into this position. "Maybe Saturday night when I leave I can take you with me."

Demi beamed. "I've missed you so much; no one else encourages me like you do. Thank you, Dixie! It means the world to me that you believe in me the way you do. It's sometimes hard when you don't have that kind of support around."

"Well, you know that I will be here no matter what," I say, quietly. Somehow, it's always felt like it's been me and Demi against the world.

Climbing into my old bed that night, I think about the day to come. I was not looking forward to it, to say the least. The last time I had seen Thelma, she was telling me to stay hopeful and keep my head up; It was going to be tough moving forward, knowing that there would be no more inspirational encouragement from the only person, other than Demi, who always seemed to understand me, and had always known exactly what to say.

The silence woke me. I hadn't realized that I was already used to the sounds of the city, but as I suddenly sat up, I had a sense that something was wrong. Looking around, one eye open and blinded by the sun beaming in through my yellow curtains at the window, brought me fully awake. I was home, and had slept in.

Glancing at the clock on the bedside table, I realized how late I'd slept: 9:45. I could smell bacon and coffee, and that hint of fresh air and grain dust that was the essence of home. That was also when I remembered that today was the day of the funeral. After a deep sign and throwing my legs over the side of the bed, I headed downstairs in search of breakfast.

The familiar sight of my Dad sitting in "his" place at the end of the table while Mom cooked breakfast in the kitchen made me smile. He glanced up from the newspaper, his coffee cup halfway to his mouth, and chuckled when he saw my messy hair and pink pajamas.

"Good morning, Dixie. How was your sleep? Did you miss your bed?"

"Good morning Dad. I think I slept well. I can't remember falling asleep and I slept in. Is there any coffee left?"

"I managed to save you some," he nodded to the carafe sitting in the middle of the table. "Mom is making breakfast."

"It smells delicious," I said to both of them, pouring myself a cup of coffee from the carafe and then reaching for the jug of orange juice. "I can't remember the last time someone made me breakfast."

"Well, you're in for a treat then. Why don't you sit and enjoy your coffee before it's ready?" My mother offered.

"Sounds great." Taking a sip of the hot brew, I sighed with contentment before opening my eyes and looking at my father as I took a seat in my old spot at the table.

"What's news in the paper this week?"

He set the paper to the side and took a sip of his coffee. "Oh, not much. The kids' volleyball season has begun and the girls won a tournament last week. They have gone forward with fixing up the old rink, and the golf course is holding a year-end tournament. Nothing overly exciting. Now, how are you?

"I forgot how comfortable my old bed was. I think I should take it back with me." I joked.

My mother turned around with a tray of bacon and eggs in hand to set on the table. "Well, I think you'll be paying a bit extra on your flight if you try to take that thing back with you. Have you seen your sister this morning? Her breakfast is getting cold."

As though she'd heard, Demi came running down the stairs.

"Is that bacon? Oh, my gosh, I love bacon. You never make me bacon anymore, Wow, I guess we know who the favourite is now, don't we?" Demi grinned as sat down in her spot at the table. "Morning everyone. Man, I slept like a full-grown man last night."

"A full-grown man?" I asked as I selected bacon from the platter.

"Whoever came up with the saying 'I slept like a baby' must have been smoking something because it makes no sense," she explained. "Babies wake up every hour and a half."

"That's very true," I laughed, glad to be home.

The next hour was spent getting ready for the funeral.

"Hey, Dix," Demi yelled from her bedroom. "Can you

come help me zip this up?"

I glanced towards the open door across the hallway from my room where I was slipping on my own dress. "Yeah, just give me a second." I hollered back as I took one last glance in the mirror and walked into the open hallway. As I headed towards Demi's room I noticed that the door to our old play room was left wide open. I paused mid step as I saw some old drawings hanging up on the wall.

"You coming?" Demi asked as she stared at me confused.

"What? Oh, yes. Just…" I walked into the play room and Demi followed curiously, holding the back of her dress so it wouldn't fall open.

"What's wrong?" She asked.

"Nothing's wrong, it's just, look at this," I pointed towards our very first vision boards that we made with Miranda and Amber and smiled a half smile. "Do you remember making these?"

Demi looked at all four pieces of paper stuck to the wall and smiled herself. "Yeah, I remember those. That was a fun day wasn't it, Dix?"

"It was." I briefly paused as I knelt and studied my own drawing. "You know, I really think Aunty Lisa was onto something when she left us that box."

"What do you mean?"

"Well, if you think about it, she left us books and movies that described how to create the life we want, right? As of now, everything I have put my heart into has come true. From originally getting the job at the retirement home, to moving away to Toronto, to this blow out with Miranda and Amber along with a handful of other things over the years. What if what Aunty said was right? What if we really *can* create our own lives to be exactly as we want? What if all of this hasn't been a coincidence? Aunty made it work, so, why can't we?"

Demi thought about it for a moment then looked at

her own drawing before running her fingers over top of the wax crayon markings. "I think you're right. We can do anything we want. We can have anything we want as well as be anything we want, and if there is ever a time of struggle we will always have each other's back." She smiled at me one more time. "The other girls might have given up on their dreams but that doesn't mean that we have to. I say we reset some new goals and make shit happen. Let's move mountains and show everyone around here that it is possible. After all, that is what Thelma wanted us to do wasn't it? So, what do you say?"

After some thought and remembering Thelma's words I stood up, adjusted my dress and stuck out my fist towards Demi. "I think that's an awesome idea. Let's do it. Now pound it and let me zip up this dress of yours."

Upon arriving at the funeral service, I found myself becoming rather emotional. After all of these years, all the visits, cups of tea, jokes, and heart-felt tidbits of advice, reality kicks in and I realized that Thelma really is gone. I sat in the car staring out the front window for an extra-long moment before Demi brought me back into reality.

"Are you going to be okay, Dix? We can wait a bit longer until everyone else is inside before we go in if you want."

After wiping away a tear and taking a deep breath I shook my head.

"No, let's go in and get this over with." I said as I climbed out of the passenger side of the car and walked inside.

We worked our way through the front doors of the church and found our place in the piers next to an older couple I recognized from town. Looking around, I realized that the place was packed; Thelma had been a very well-known and respected woman in town. As I look around, I see a few rows in front of us, Miranda and Amber, who are sitting with their respective parents. I assume their mothers made them come so I smiled a soft, sad smile of greeting and all I received in return was a set of eye rolls and a sneer. It would appear that Demi was serious when she said not to bother. I do feel as though I deserve an explanation though, seeing as I haven't done anything wrong. They were supposed to be my best friends, weren't they?

The service went on for about forty-five minutes after which everyone slowly left the building and headed towards the hall for snacks and a presentation that had been made about Thelma and her life. Demi and I had waited outside, once our tears had finally dried up, until the girls slowly made their way from inside. After some deep breathing, I decided to take a stand and confront Miranda and Amber head on.

"Hey, do you guys have a second? I need to talk to you," I boldly asked whilst walking towards the two girls.

"What do you want Dixie?" Miranda snarled back as they continued walking.

"Miranda, I need to clear this up between us. Whatever this is that is going on between you and I has got to end. I mean, we have been best friends for years. I don't understand why you are holding such a grudge towards me and spreading such horrible rumors."

Miranda and Amber both stopped walking and spun around to face us. My heart skipped a beat as I could see the hurt and anger in Miranda's eyes. "You don't understand? Seriously Dixie. After everything you've done to hurt and betray us, you're honestly asking me this right now?"

"What are you talking about?" I demanded, genuinely confused. "I left to further my own career and life. How is that a betrayal of you?"

"You're a real piece of work, you know that?" Miranda spat bitterly. "For years, all we ever talked about was having each other's back and being there for one another no matter what. And then out of the blue you decide that this," Miranda spread her arms out. "Us, isn't good enough for you anymore, so you move off with a last-minute notice. How do you think that made me feel, Dixie?" Miranda's eyes began to swell with tears. "You literally broke my heart. I thought that we were closer than that. How do we deserve to be treated as though we are nothing to you?"

My heart then sank even further and a lump begun to grow in my throat when she told me her true feelings. "I had no idea that my leaving would hurt you the way that it did, Miranda. I figured that seeing as we weren't children anymore, you would understand that there is more to life than what we had previously lived. Do you not want more than what this town has to offer? Don't you want to see what else is out there for you?" Glancing over at Amber, I offer a form of sympathy. "You guys do know that it is okay to want more than this right? There's nothing wrong with wanting that or wanting to at least know what is out there."

"We get that, Dixie," Amber offered. "We just don't get why you had to keep your desire a secret for so long. Why couldn't you just tell us your plans sooner? You clearly planned leaving long before you did, but you refused to give us a heads up until practically the last minute. We just want to know why."

"I told you guys before, I honestly didn't think you would understand. My biggest fear through all of this was that you guys wouldn't get it. I was petrified that you would hate me for wanting more. That you would think I was abandoning you or something. I need you guys to know that I never wanted this." Tears begun to form in my eyes. "I care about you two more than you could ever imagine. All I wanted was for you to be happy for me. I was praying for well wishes and potential visits whenever I would come home, but instead I have *this* to come home to. I never meant to hurt you two. You have to believe me."

Miranda put her head down and gazed at the sidewalk, biting the inside of her cheek before looking back up at myself and Demi. "You might not have meant to hurt us Dixie, but you did. You broke our hearts and that's not something that can be repaired overnight. I'm sorry that you feel the need for more, but we are happy here in this town. Not all of us need to go out and achieve our dreams to be happy. Sometimes you have to open your eyes to reality and live the life you were handed. This is life Dixie, small town Moville and the jobs that are available here. Not some crazy fantasy job that would be practically impossible to get. I'm never going to be a surgeon, Dixie, just like Amber won't own a chain of hotels and you likely won't ever become an actual author. You need to get your head out of the clouds and come back down to earth with the rest of us. You are only making yourself look foolish, everyone in town says so."

I tried to process everything Miranda had just told me but all I could think about then was the rumors she had spread about me. "So it is true," I stared intently into her eyes.

"What?" Miranda questioned, clearly confused.

"That you guys had been talking about me with others around here. You *had* been spreading the rumors," I look over to Amber, who then put her head down in defeat. "You know, I really thought that there was a slight chance of us fixing our relationship, but how can I continue to fight for a friendship that no longer exists?"

Miranda crossed her arms and lifted her head, ready for another argument.

"Wow," I state, clearly hurt. "You both know that I never left here to chase after some guy and the fact that you two would say such things really twists the knife that you placed in my back."

Looking around at the people walking by on the streets, headed towards the hall reminded me of the advice

Thelma had given me just a few weeks prior. I looked back at Miranda and Amber, "You know, a wise woman once said that if someone is your true friend, they will stand by your side no matter what decision you make in life and that that friend would be honestly happy for you. It's clear to me now that you two aren't the friends that I thought you were... So, again, I am sorry that I hurt you in all of this and I'm sorry that I didn't tell you sooner about my decision to leave, but I don't deserve to continuously be treated this way. If you don't want to be friends any longer, then I will accept that and move on because I'm not going to stand here and beg for a relationship, but you need to know that this isn't what I want. This right here, is your decision and you can accept my apology or not... You have my number if you ever want to talk again."

I nodded towards Demi who stood nervous and wide-eyed beside me. "I think it's time to head on into the hall, it looks like almost everyone is inside already." After one last glance at the girls, I said "good bye," linked arms with Demi and walked over to the hall where we would find our seats and watch the presentation on Thelma's life.

Once the presentation was over and everyone was moved to tears in their seats, a middle-aged woman came up behind me and placed her hand on my shoulder.

"Excuse me, Dixie?" She said cautiously.

Demi and I both turned around in our seats curious. "Yes?" I asked.

"Oh, good. It is you, it's been so long since I've seen you last that I wasn't sure if I had the right person or not. You've grown so much."

That was when I recognized the woman as Thelma's daughter, Melissa. I had met her a handful of times when she would come to have supper with her mother at the retirement home. I smiled a genuine smile and stood to give her a hug. "Hey Melissa, I am so sorry for your loss. How are you holding up?"

"Oh you know, as good as one can be under the circumstances. It's just hard to wrap my head around Mom actually being gone, you know?"

"I totally get it. But I'm sure it will only get easier with time."

"Yeah, I've heard that a few times before… so, um, I have something for you." She choked back some tears and handed me a white envelope with my name written on the front and a stamp in the top right corner. By a quick glance I could tell that it was Thelma's writing.

Curious, I asked her, "What is this?"

"Honestly, I'm not sure. I found it on Mom's counter and didn't think it was my place to open it but rather deliver it to its rightful owner." She gave a half smile.

"Well, thank you, Melissa. I appreciate it."

"You're welcome. Now, I better get moving on, I have a few other people that I need to talk to before this is all over. You take care, okay?"

"I will, and you do the same. Thank you again."

Melissa left to talk to someone else a few meters away and I sat down at our table, only this time staring at the letter in hand.

"What do you think it is?" Demi asked.

"I'm not sure," I reply. "But I don't think I can open it right now. I've dealt with enough today, and don't want to cry anymore. What do you say we head home?"

Demi gave me a side shoulder hug. "Sounds good to me."

We grabbed our purses as well as the white envelope and headed out of the hall towards home.

Upon arriving to our parents' house, we changed into more comfortable clothes, and because we were home, and we knew our parents would be home to supervise Demi, we poured ourselves each a glass of wine and sat down in the living room, next to the fireplace and waited until our parents came home half an hour later with pizza and ice

105

cream in hand.

Sitting on the couch, holding my glass of wine I looked up at my Mother. "Mom, can I ask you something?"

Mid-bite of pizza, she replied. "Yes, of course you can. What is it?"

"Why is it that some people change in the way that they do?" I asked as I slowly took another sip from my glass and nibble on my own piece of pizza. "I mean, what exactly makes a person change? I told you about Miranda and Amber and I honestly don't understand why they are still so upset with me."

She thought about it for a few seconds before replying.

"You know, hun, that's a really tricky question to answer. I wouldn't say that it's the same for everyone as to what makes them change. It all depends on what occurs in a person's life and how they choose to handle it. Example, when Lisa passed away, I had become very quiet and reserved as I'm sure you both remember." Demi and I both nodded. "I was not in a good place emotionally for a very long time and it took me a few years and to lose multiple clients as well as interior decorating jobs, to break out of that dark place and become the healthy person, both physically and mentally, that I am today. I understand that I am still not the same person that I was when Lisa was around. I'm still not as outgoing and bubbly as I once was but going through that tragedy, it has made me change. It was the loss of her that made me lose sight of who I was, which turned me into another person for that period of time. Do you see where I am going with this? A person will react to things in their own way. Everyone is different and all you can do is pray that they react in a healthy manner.

"One day I woke up after Lisa was gone and I took a good long hard look at my life and where not only myself, but you two and your father were at in it. I was not happy and neither were all of you because of how I had dealt with it. I let myself become severely depressed and refused to put any effort into anything. It wasn't until one day, a few years after her passing, that I realized my life would never be fulfilled again until I allowed myself to be happy. You see, happiness is an internal thing that no one on the outside can control. After realizing how miserable I was, I decided to get out of bed every day with good intentions in mind. I make small goals for myself in the morning to help keep me going. Life is only as hard as you make it, don't ever forget that, alright, girls?"

We both nodded again. "Okay Mom, we will remember that." I replied.

"But as for the girls, I really do believe that jealousy is playing a big role in all of this. Let's look at the big picture. You all went camping a while back and were enjoying yourselves until you mentioned you would be leaving. The girls then got upset and hurt by your not telling them sooner. That is understandable, yes?"

"Yeah," I replied again.

"Okay, so, first they have the hurt set in and as time goes on they see that you are, in fact, leaving and heading off to somewhere that they could only dream of going, as well. Correct?"

"Correct."

"Then, they hear through the grape vine that you are doing alright for yourself and are happy where you chose to live. Do you think for one minute that isn't going to sting a bit? These girls had dreams just as big as yours, only they chose not to fulfil theirs. They lost track somewhere along the way and forgot where they were headed. But you didn't and that is what upsets them today and is the reason they act the way they do. Miranda and Amber don't know how to control their jealousy because, well, they are young yet. Once they learn how to control it they might be happy for you, but until then there is a chance that they will want you to fail because that way they could tell you *I told you so*. But you won't fail now, will you?"

"I hope not."

"No, you won't fail. You are going to continue pushing and fighting until you achieve your wildest dreams. Anyone who matters to you will be there with you until the end. Got it?"

I sat and stared into the fireplace as it popped and crackled.

"Thank you for your honest answer." I smiled. "I suppose that all make sense. I just wish they would be even a little more supportive, but you can't control anyone's emotions but your own, right?"

"Exactly,"

"Hmm, well, there we go then."

We all sat in silence for a few minutes as we finished up our supper before I restarted the conversation.

"Um, so this is completely off topic from before, but while we have you here, do you think that we can talk about Demi for a moment?"

Both of our parents glanced at each other while Demi looked over at me with hope in her eyes.

"What about Demi?" My father questioned hesitantly.

"Well, I know that she had mentioned to you guys the idea of moving in with me and finishing her last year or so by correspondence. I was just wondering where you were at with the idea…"

Chapter Twelve

"Oh my goodness Dix, this place is amazing!" Demi exclaimed as we made our way into my small, one bedroom apartment. "It's so cute in here. Um, where should I put my bags?" Demi asked as she took a look around the room. "Oh, my goodness, are those the candles that Grandma gave you?" She pointed to a shelf above the couch. "They are so much prettier than I remember."

"Yeah, they are. I can't bring myself to burn them because they are so gorgeous. You can set your bags over on the couch for now. We will fold it out and you can sleep there until you get a job and we can find a bigger place."

She rolled her bag to the living room and laid it on the floor off to the side and out of the way. "Dix, can you believe that we are both here right now?" she asked as she began to walk around the apartment, examining each of the small rooms.

I smiled as I reached into the fridge and grabbed us each a bottle of water before tossing Demi one. "I know, this is so unreal. I am surprised Mom and Dad let you come. I'll be honest. I hoped they would agree to letting you come, but I wasn't holding my breath."

"I know. I was the same, actually. I dreamt of this since the day you left and I replayed versions of the outcome of the conversation with Mom and Dad every night before I fell asleep, just like I've done with everything else I wanted growing up…" She smiled. "I knew they would let me come live with you. I just knew it."

"Well, I'm glad they did. This is the beginning of our forever," I smiled back. "Okay, so first things first. We need to make you a new resume or at least touch up your old one. As for your schooling stuff, Mom said that she would mail it all out here as soon as she got it and yeah," I exhaled deeply. "Let's get you settled in. I'll show you around so you get to know the place, although, I think you've already seen most of it."

Later that evening, after Demi was organized, we headed out for supper at one of my favorite restaurants a few blocks over. We had just sat down with a menu and glass of water when my phone rang an unidentified number.

"Hello, is this Dixie Churn by chance?"

"This is she," I reply, hesitant.

"Oh, wonderful, this is Penelope Burberry from R&R publishing."

I held my breath tight and my eyes widened as Demi looked at me clearly confused. I had briefly mentioned Naomi's offer to my family during one of our sit-down meals, but told them that it wasn't a for sure deal. So, when I mouthed the words 'my book', Demi's eyes widened as well. "I have read your story and would like to have a meeting with you tomorrow afternoon if that is at all possible?"

My heart began to beat even faster.

"Oh, um wow yes, absolutely," I stutter. "Can I ask for a time and a place? I can come anywhere, anytime. Tomorrow's schedule is wide open for me."

"How does 10:45 am at 216 Spadina sound? I will be in my office so if you tell the receptionist that we have a meeting, she will direct you in."

"That-that sounds perfect. Thank you so much!"

"Alight, we will see you then."

Her end went dead as she hung up the phone and I looked at Demi in both, shock and amazement.

"What? What did they say?" Demi demanded.

I stared at Demi momentarily as I let the phone call sink in before I replied.

"I'm not sure, she just said that she wants to meet

with me. Oh, my goodness, I need to text Naomi and let her know. Hey, is it alright if she meets us back at home? I'll see if she's free."

"Yeah, go for it. I can't wait to meet her." Demi glanced up and quickly asked, "The waitress is coming, do you know what you want? I'll order while you do that."

"Please, I'll just have the grilled chicken burger and a side Ceasar salad. Thanks." I quickly messaged Naomi and she agreed to meet us back at our apartment in roughly an hour.

"…and I'll have the garden salad with grilled chicken. Thank you." The waitress smiled and walked away from our table while Demi looked at me. "I really need to start eating better if I'm going to begin my modeling journey soon." She smiled. "So… is she going to meet us or what?"

"Yes, she said she can meet us at the apartment in about an hour. So, once we are done eating our meal we will get some dessert to go and head back. I think you will like her, Dem. I've only met her twice now and she has already helped me so much."

"She sounds wonderful."

After completing our meal and discussing work arrangements and opportunities, ground rules for the apartment as well as casual talk, we took off with cheesecake in hand; back to the apartment, where Naomi was walking up to the door to ring the buzzer.

"Oh, my gosh, I'm so sorry you beat us back. We tried to hurry as fast as we could. How long have you been here?" I asked as I raced to get my keys out of my pocket.

"No, worries," Naomi dismissed my concern. "I literally just got to the steps as you came around the corner. I hadn't buzzed yet. How was supper?" she asked cheerfully.

"It was amazing, once again. I got my usual chicken burger and salad. Demi here had some salad with chicken.

Did you eat yet? Oh, and by the way, this is my sister, Demi. She is now living with me."

"Pleasure to meet you, Demi. I'm Naomi." She extended her right arm and shook hands with Demi.

"Pleasures all mine," Demi replied.

"Yes, I did eat. I had a wrap and some soup before I left my place."

"Oh, good," I was relieved that she didn't miss her supper due to us. "The door's unlocked. Let's head up there." We hurried up multiple sets of stairs and when we finally reached my tiny apartment, I set our cheesecake and purse on the counter while the girls settled in on the couch. I then turned to Naomi and told her the great news.

"So, I have no idea what you did, but Penelope Burberry wants to meet me tomorrow in person to talk about my book. Isn't that amazing? Seriously, Naomi, if this all goes through I owe you my life."

"Are you serious? That was so fast!" she exclaimed. "I mean, that's awesome but I didn't think it would happen so quickly. Yay!"

"I know, I wasn't holding my breath on it mostly because I haven't had any luck anywhere else but, wow, my mind is blown."

The rest of the evening was spent discussing what life would be like if my book became a best seller, along with all the opportunities ahead. The time went by and before too long it was midnight and we decided that it was too late for Naomi to get a ride so we all snuggled into my bed and fell asleep.

The next morning came in a rush when we woke around 8:20 am.

"Oh Lord. You guys get up!" I startled both girls. "It's almost 8:30 and we all need to eat and get ready."

I rolled over top of Demi and fell to the floor with a 'thud'. I started to laugh. "Agh! I'm okay! Come on guys I need help finding something to wear. I only have an hour to leave and if you guys are coming with me then we need to hurry."

I raced to the bathroom to wash my face and turned on my hair straightener. By the time I came back out, the girls were sitting up with one eye open. "Well, good morning to you guys. Okay, so I was thinking I could either wear the same dress I wore to Thelma's funeral or I have this navy-blue dress and my black blazer. Maybe accent it with gold? What do you think?"

Demi yawned and slid out of bed and headed toward the coffee maker where she began to make a pot. "I think the blue and black blazer sounds great," she shuffled through the cupboards. "Where's the coffee?"

"Left cupboard, on the top shelf," I replied as I started to get dressed.

Naomi then crawled out of bed and began to get dressed as well. "Are you always such a morning person, Dixie? I've never seen someone so chipper first thing in the morning before."

Demi giggled, "She's been a morning person since, what? Birth? At home, she's always been the first person up and ready to go before anyone else in the house."

"Hey, what can I say? Mornings are the best part of the day."

Both Naomi and Dixie stopped what they were doing to stare at me doubtfully.

"Yeah, okay Dix. Whatever you say," Demi finished making her coffee.

The entire next hour was mayhem while we raced around to get ready and get a small amount of food into us. When we were all set, we grabbed our bags and headed down the flights of stairs and headed out the front of the building where we scurried to the subway and headed off to my meeting.

The whole ride there felt like an eternity.

"Dix, you need to calm down, it's going to be fine. If you keep worrying like this I think you will sweat right though that blazer," Naomi handed me a napkin from her purse.

"Thanks," I dabbed my hair line and the back of my neck. "I'm just so nervous. This is just such a big deal to me. I can't even explain it anymore. And It doesn't help that it feels like it's taking forever to get there," my voice rose in panic.

"We should be there any minute. Now, Dixie, look at me." Naomi grabbed my face from her seat next to me. "You are going to go in there and rock this thing okay? You have worked too hard to give up and no matter what the outcome, Demi and I will be in the waiting room for you. So, sit up straight, take a deep breath and hold on tight because the rest of your life is waiting for you."

The subway train pulled to a halt. Taking a deep breath, my friends by my side, I exited the subway and made my way towards the building that potentially held my future.

* * *

"So, how did it go?" Demi asked as I came out of the office in which my meeting was held. I walked towards them with a saddened look on my face. That is, until I got right next to them when I squeaked, "They want to publish it!"

"What? OH, MY GOSH!" Naomi and Demi said almost a little too loudly, as the receptionist looked up in our direction. They then lowered their tone. "Dixie, that's fantastic! I knew you could do it. What did she say?" Naomi asked.

"Well, they first needed my signature and all that fun stuff to make it official and then they said they are going to send it off to editing right away and then we might need to add and fix up a few areas but overall she really liked my story. Only, she told me that I need to find myself an agent for future reference. Apparently, they won't accept any work unless it goes through an agent first, so I am lucky that she even took the time to look at my work. Thank your friend for me okay, Naomi? I have another meeting with her next week to talk about everything in detail. Wow, I can hardly breathe right now, this is finally happening! You guys...I'm going to officially be an author! After all the crap, I've dealt with from having such a hard time finding a publisher, to dealing with the girls back home, to Thelma passing away, to all the other little things that have gone on, I think I'm finally getting my break. I guess there is such thing as good karma when you try your absolute hardest and always be the bigger person. You know, if it wasn't for you Naomi, none of this would have happened."

I reached over and gave Naomi a hug, tears streaming down my cheeks. The relief I was feeling was indescribable.

"You are totally right. You have gone through a lots this summer and it's about time that the universe started working in your favor. Holy man, Dix, we need to celebrate."

"Who are you texting?" I asked with a confused look on my face.

"Logan. I told him I would tell him the news if you got it or not. I think that we should all go out for supper and celebrate."

"Whoa, whoa, whoa, you're still talking to Logan? When were you planning on telling me this? You haven't mentioned it once in weeks!"

"Wait, who's Logan?" Naomi asked, clearly confused.

"He's a guy we met earlier this summer. Things clicked with him and I while Dixie was talking to his friend, Turner. They both live here in the city somewhere and I think it's be fun to meet up with them and share the great news."

"Uhm, okay yeah lets to it," Naomi looked at me.

"What do you say, author lady?"

After a moment of thought, I spout out "I say, heck yes! Tonight, we are going out for supper and I am buying your meal and drinks as a small thank you."

"Oh, Dixie, you don't have to do that. Really, it's the least I could do. I've already been given two new friends. I don't need anything else," She paused and smiled. "I think that this is going to be a beautiful friendship. Now, who wants to go do some shopping to get this celebration started? We will need new outfits if we are going to meet these handsome men you two seem to know. You should see if they have an extra friend so I'm not a fifth wheel!"

"Already on it." Demi piped up. "Logan mentioned it to Turner just now and they said they can meet us at 5:00pm anywhere we want and they have a buddy they said they can bring. So, you guys ready? Let's get our shop on. I think I need something red to start my city collection."

With that we all linked arms and made our way out of the building and down the street amongst all the other city dwellers and the hundreds of businesses and shops that flooded the streets.

Chapter Thirteen

I should have known that things were going too well in my favor; the start of the very next week, my landlord was banging on my door before the rest of the city was awake, questioning how long my "guest" would be staying, and informing me that my rental agreement stated no roommates. Demi and I had to find a new place to live. Like, now.

After a wine-fuelled talk about it that evening Naomi, Demi and I decided to find a place to rent together. It took a month but we found a place big enough for us all to fit, live comfortably as well as affordably. It was a small two bedroom, one bathroom house that was a little outdated but overall, worked for us. Demi and I shared one room while Naomi took the other. The only problem lately was keeping up with our jobs to make sure that our share of the rent was paid for.

Demi finished her home schooling within a few short months and went back home to take her tests, which she passed with flying colors. She had also been landing a few small modeling gigs here and there within the city, but not enough to make any serious money, so she continued to work at a clothing store downtown to make ends meet.

Naomi had been working at a restaurant about twenty minutes from our new house during the day as well as at a bar in the evenings. She hated both jobs but did them anyway until she could find something a little more suited for her.

As for myself, well, I was struggling with my writing… a lot. My first book had been published and, so far, was doing alright. I had made some money with it but not enough to keep my bank account where I hoped it would have been and I hadn't made the best sellers list either.

I had still been seeing Turner, but due to us both having such busy schedules, we hadn't seen each other as much as one would expect from a new relationship. Needless to say, that began to take a toll on the both of us and added to the pile of stress in my life, not to mention my job at the café had been cut down to part time, unfortunately.

I was working there three days a week, rather than five to six like I used to so, to fill in some of my spare time when I wasn't writing, I began to volunteer at woman's shelter downtown. It didn't pay anything, obviously, but it did give me a feeling of purpose. I had met a lot of women who had very interesting stories to share and it left me with the feeling that I had to help as much as I could. I had been very blessed in this life time not to struggle like so many other women did so to pay it forward, I did all that I could to help them get back on their feet.

I would host meetings once a week to teach women how the laws of attraction work and what they could do, say and think, to help further their own lives. I've begun to research quantum physics and how it all works on a deeper level that what I had previously learned. And after learning all that I did on the topic of energy, you would think that I would be living the life. Instead, the hole I seemed to be in, kept getting bigger and bigger every time I turned around.

"Dix, I'm home," Demi yelled as she walked through the front door, towards the kitchen for a bottle of water.

"I see that, you didn't have to shout," I mumbled under my breath. "How was your run?" I asked as I set my laptop to the side on the couch.

"So hot. It must be over thirty degrees out there," she said as she wiped beads of sweat off her brow. "What are you working on today?" She then sat down with her legs crossed on our new lounging chair to the side of me.

"Oh, just some new book ideas and an article about

the struggles of being an author that I'm going to submit to a magazine." I paused and began to rub my forehead in distress. "I've hit a block lately, Dem. I've never been more confused on what to write about in my life. Normally it just comes to me, but lately I've drawn a blank and it's driving me crazy…" I paused again, only this time to wipe the tears off my face.

"Oh, Dix, it'll be alright. You'll come up with something." Demi came over to the couch and gave me a hug.

"No, it's not just that. I got dropped by my agent this morning."

Demi's eyes widened as she became speechless. "What? Why?"

"Because apparently, I haven't given them what they want so they told me that they had to let me go. Dem, I've given them five different manuscripts. I've put hours upon hours of work into everything I've written and it's still not good enough. I'm so frustrated and annoyed and ugh!" I spout clearly upset. "I… I just don't know what to do. Do you know how hard it was to get the agent I did have? Now what am I going to do?"

"Oh, Dix, you'll figure it out, you always do. Maybe there's a different way to get your work out?"

"I don't know. So now not only do I only work two, maybe three days a week but now there's this. What the hell am I going to do for money now?" I sob into my knees as I continue to sit on the couch.

Just then Naomi came barreling thought the door like a kid on Christmas morning. "Hey guys guess wha-…" She froze in her place once she saw me crying on the couch. "Oh, my God. What's wrong? Are you okay, Dixie?" She dropped her purse on the floor and hurried to my side. As she sat on the couch with Demi and I she asked, "Seriously, what is it?" She demanded.

"Dix got let go by her agent today," Demi calmly replied.

"Oh, no. Why? Your first book went over so well, why would they let you go now?"

I lifted my head, mascara streaming down my cheeks. "Because my work apparently sucks. They haven't liked my past five submissions." I wiped my face with my hands.

"Oh, come now. You know that your work doesn't suck, Dix," Naomi offered. "Maybe you just don't have the right agent. Maybe there's a better one out their waiting for someone like you."

"Yeah, okay," I mumbled and took a deep breath to calm myself. "I don't know, maybe coming here was a bad idea. I thought I could do it. I thought I could be like Aunt Lisa and make something of myself, but instead, ever since I moved to this city all I've gotten was a craptastic job and then managed to get cut down from full time to part-time. I published one book, but hardly anything to show for it, I got kicked out of my original apartment, and now, dropped by my agent. What could honestly go wrong next?"

"Dixie, you take that back right now!" Demi demanded. "You don't want to attract anything else to go wrong, now do you? You're asking the universe what could go wrong. Don't give it a chance to answer."

"Ugh! Fine, I take it back. I'm just… frustrated. And after all of this, Turner has been on my case lately about not giving our relationship enough attention."

"What?" they both say at almost the same time, clearly confused.

"Yeah, we haven't hung out much because he's usually working, or I'm either working at the café or volunteering at the shelter and if not, I'm working on my writing. We've seen each other once in almost three weeks. Like, we text and call each other, but lately we have been very distant and he's getting a little upset. I just have had so much on my plate; it doesn't seem like he understands the pressure that I'm under lately. Like, I can't expect you two to cover all of the bills in this house."

"Oh, well, I'm sure he will get over it. Maybe you two need to take a day to have to yourselves and explain all of this to him. I think you need to get out of this house anyway. After the morning you are having, a date might do you good." Naomi offered.

"Yeah, maybe," I think about it for a moment. "I'll give him a call and see what he's doing tonight."

"That's my girl. I'll even help you do your hair and pick something nice out for you to wear."

"Thanks, Nai. Thanks, Dem. You two always know how to make me feel better," I wiped my dripping nose on the sleeve of my shirt. "Ugh, this sucks." I begin to laugh as the mood lightens.

"It'll get better, it always does. Just picture your final outcome and how you want things to turn out." Demi reminded me.

"Good point. I teach this stuff every week and all of my writing revolves around this topic, why is it that I struggle so much sometimes with it?" I lean back into the couch.

"Because, you are human. Everyone struggles at the best of times," Demi replied back. "You don't think Oprah struggled at some point in her life and career? What about Ellen DeGeneres? I'm sure she did too, and J.K Rowling? Dix, it's a part of life. Each of these hurdles are making you stronger and teaching you new lessons every time.

"You can't give up though, not only are your readers looking up to you, but so are all of those incredible women at the shelter. You give them hope every single time you go into that building. You give them strength by what you teach them on the laws of attraction. You're struggling now, but it's not too late to change your way of thinking and straighten this all out, now is it?"

I stare ahead of me as I process everything she just said. "I guess you're right. I need to stop having this pity party for myself and figure out my next step to dig my way out of this mess." I rubbed my forehead.

"Why don't you go have a shower, do your hair and make-up and give Turner a call. I bet you'll feel a lot better once you get out of those pyjamas," Naomi rubbed my shoulder.

"Okay, I'll do that. Thanks, guys." I give them both thankful looks as I climb off the couch. "Wait a minute, what's your news?" I look back at Naomi.

"What?" she asked.

"When you came in, you were all bouncy and excited about something, what was it?"

"Oh!" She exclaimed. "I was going to tell you guys about my new job offer. But, I figured maybe this wasn't the best time seeing as what you were going through and such."

"You got a new job offer?" Demi squeaked. "Where? As what?"

"Downtown, as a realtor's assistant. I mentioned to a guy I work with at the bar, that I wanted to be a realtor one day and he told me that his brother was looking for an assistant. He then told me to send in a resume and he'd put in a good word. Well, after a week or so, I finally got a phone call to go in for a meeting this morning and well, I got the job!"

As happy as I was for Naomi, my heart sunk a little. How is it that while I'm going through all this crap in my life, that Naomi seems to be succeeding so effortlessly. It just doesn't seem fair. But, knowing what I know, the happier you are for someone, opens gateways for yourself so, I brought myself out of my gloomy state, smiled and congratulated her on the opportunity she received before heading for a shower.

The rest of the day dragged on until about five o'clock, when all three of us girls sat around the living room which was covered in make-up, curling irons, hair spray and a variety of other beauty products.

"Thank you both for doing this for me today. I really appreciate it." I said as I sat in a chair in the middle of the room while Demi worked on applying my makeup and Naomi curled and teased my hair.

"No worries, you deserve it." Naomi replied.

"Plus, its super fun for us. It's like playing makeup all over again, isn't it, Dix. Remember when we would play with Mom's all the time?"

I smiled. "Yeah, I remember. That was fun."

"Agreed," she said as she began to contour my face. "Only, now we actually know what we are doing."

"You two sound like you were the cutest kids on the planet. I wish I had a sister growing up to do that sort of things with," Naomi sighed.

"It was great. But hey, now you have us instead," Demi beamed.

"That's very true. And I wouldn't trade you both for the world."

We all smiled and the girls continued dressing me up.

"So, what time did Turner say he was coming?" Naomi asked after several minutes.

"Um, Roughly six or shortly after. He said he managed to make reservations somewhere for 6:45pm. So, we have less than an hour to finish up getting ready. I still need to find an outfit to wear as well."

"Well don't worry, we will find you something. Turner won't know what hit him by the time we are done with you."

Demi smirked. "He won't be able to keep his hands to himself either."

"Well good, maybe it will help get us over this hump we seem to be at."

Just then, my cell phone began to ring. Naomi quickly grabbed it off the counter and handed it to me. "It says *Mom*," she said.

Demi and myself looked at each other both confused and curious.

"Hello." I answered.

"Hi Hun, is Demi with you?" My mom asked quickly.

"Yeah, hold on, I'll put you on speaker phone." I pressed the screen so we could all hear. "Okay, you're on. What's going on?"

"Girls, I need you both to come home as soon as you can. Your father had been hit by a semi while on his way home from the city today. He is in the hospital in Winnipeg right now." She began to sob on the other end. "They haven't told me exactly how bad he is yet, but they say it doesn't look good. All I know is that he has broken multiple bones and when the first responders arrived he was unconscious. He is in surgery as we speak," she took a deep breath to calm herself. "Please come home. He needs to see you."

All three of us froze in place as we look at one another in horror.

"Did you hear me?" My mother asked on the other end.

"Uh, yeah. W-we heard you. Mom. I... We will catch a flight first thing in the morning. I'll see if there's anything going out tonight though. Mom, tell me he will be okay."

I began to cry, ruining all the hard work Demi just did putting on my make-up and just as I did, Demi began to cry as well as she reached to hold my hand.

"I've been praying that he will be ever since I got a phone call. I can't lose him, too. Just come home. Okay? Text me or call me when you land. I'll meet you in the waiting room when you do and if there are any changes I will let you both know."

"Okay, Mom?"

"Yes?"

"We love you," I say, hardly able to speak.

"Tell Daddy that we are coming and to stay strong," Demi spouted out.

"I will, just hurry okay?" Mom asked.

"Okay, see you tomorrow."

"Okay, fly safe. I love you both so much."

We then hung up the phone and Demi broke down crying in a way I have never seen before. I got off my chair and helped her up and hugged her tightly. Naomi then turned off the curling iron and got her own phone out to check for upcoming flights to Winnipeg.

"It'll be alright," I whisper as I hold her head, my own tears running into her hair. "Let's hurry and go pack our bags and we will get out of here as soon as we can. Oh, crap! Turner!" I gasped. "I need to call Turner now. And work! Oh, my God. Demi, you have tomorrow off, right?"

"Yeah," she sobbed as she flung the closet door open.

"Okay, and I don't work until the day after tomorrow. I'll call and get more time off when we get home and you can do the same."

"Okay, I'm sure they will understand."

"There's a flight heading out in two and a half hours," Naomi blurted out as Demi and myself ran around packing and sifting through the closet in our bedroom for a suitcase.

"Oh, my Lord! We need to hurry. Dem, you quickly pack what we all need, I'll call Turner and then let's get out of here. Nai, I assume you'll be alright if we go?"

"Don't you worry about me, you two have places to be. Just keep me posted, alright?"

"Okay, we will." I then called Turner and told him that I wouldn't be able to make it to supper due to our father being admitted to the hospital. He was obviously disappointed, but fully understood and supported my decision to leave.

The cab drive to the airport felt like eternity, but once there we managed to catch a flight with minutes to spare. Both Demi and I settled in in one of the seats closer to the front and wiped away more tears.

"It's going to be alright." I said, "Ask, believe, receive, right? Dad will be fine. He is healthy and healing the way he should. Let's send him some love and light."

"Okay," Demi whispered as she grabbed a hold of my hand.

We both closed our eyes, took a deep breath and imagined loving, healing energy as well as light going towards our father, hours away.

Chapter Fourteen

We arrived at the Winnipeg hospital sometime in the early hours of the morning. We hadn't looked at any clocks, for we hurried as fast as we could to the hospital. Upon arriving, we found our mother in tears in the waiting room, pacing back and forth.

"Mom!" Demi cried as she raced towards her, luggage bag in hand. "How is he? Tell me he is going to be alright." She then dropped her suit case and embraced our mother tightly.

"Oh, my girls. Come here." I then reached her and got in on the hug. "They said that his left leg was broken just below the knee as well as his left arm and he had a crack in three of his ribs, plus some head trauma, but they said he will be alright. They were moving him into surgery and told me to wait down here until they came to get me." She gently wiped away one of Demi's tears.

"Thank God," I said as I let out a deep, relieved breath. I guess sending all of that love and light really did help. "We raced here as soon as you called. We managed to get a flight just in time and got a cab from the airport to get here. I've never been more worried in my life. How are you holding up?"

"Well, now that I know he will be alright and you girls are both here, I will be fine. I've been sick since the afternoon when I got the call. It's just not something you ever want to hear, especially since losing Lisa in a similar way. It felt as though I was living it all over again."

"Well, he's fine, so let's take a deep breath and sit down until they come to get us," I suggested.

We all agreed and took a seat in some of the open seats in the center of the waiting area. After talking and napping for roughly two and a half hours, a nurse came through a set of doors, calling my mother's name.

"Doreen Churn?" The nurse called and my mother quickly stood up to face her, waking Demi, who was asleep on her shoulder. "Your husband is waiting for you," she smiled.

"Thank you," my mother replied. "Are you girls coming? I'm sure he will want to see you just as much."

Demi and I grabbed our bag that we decided to share and followed the nurse and our mother down various hallways to the recovery room.

"Daddy!" Demi squeaked and raced to his bedside to give him a hug.

"Hi, baby. How are my girls doing?" He asked as he winced in pain from Demi's quick embrace.

"Oops, sorry," she said.

"No worries. How are you? Hi, Hun," he smiled at our mom. "Well, I was on my way home," he chuckled.

"Don't ever do that to me again," she replied sternly as she grabbed hold of his hand. "You had me worried sick. How are you feeling?" She wiped away another tear.

"Well, they gave me some pain meds, but I still don't feel too hot, that's for sure."

"The main thing is that you are alive. The pain will eventually subside."

You could tell by the look in both of my parents' eyes, that they loved each other more than life itself and the thought of losing one or the other would kill their very soul.

"That's true. Now, how did you girls get here so fast? Don't you have work tomorrow? Today? What time is it?" he asked both Demi and myself.

"No," I responded. "We both have tomorrow off and we are going to call our bosses once we get home. I mean, to your house, to get more time off. And it's around eight o'clock, I think. When do you get to go home?"

"I'm not sure, they figure I won't be here long, though. I'd like to go home as soon as possible."

Just then a nurse came through the curtain to check on our father and see how he was doing and told him that he would likely be able to go home in a day or two. The rest of the day passed as all four of us bonded and comforted one another after the almost tragedy that just took place.

Our mom stayed in Winnipeg with Dad, and Demi and I were sent to the farm to get some rest and a meal. While our parents were away, over the course of two days, Demi and I cleaned the entire house, baked various treats, and bought a big bouquet of brightly colored flowers from the local flower shop, that would sit in the center of the table.

While cleaning, I discovered a white envelope in one of the kitchen drawers. On the front, it had my name and address written on it. That was when I remembered that it was the letter Thelma's daughter gave me after the funeral. Curious, I carefully opened it.

Dear Dixie,

I hope that things are going well for you. It's been a while since I last wrote so I wanted to let you know that everything is going wonderfully here. Demi has caught on to the swing of things about as fast as you did. The rest of the residents love her to pieces and talk about what a wonderful young lady she is. I hope that you are doing just as well. I want you to remember that even though life gets tough sometimes, you can't give up. Starting anything new is going to take time and patience but as time goes on, you will see that it's not as hard as you once thought it was. Take care, my dear.

XO- Thelma

I slowly placed the letter back in the envelope and stared into thin air for the next five minutes remembering all the great times I had with Thelma, as well as all her inspiring words of wisdom. After I collected my thoughts, I called Turner to let him know that our dad was alright and would be home in no time.

"That's great news," he replied, "How banged up was he?"

"He had a broken leg, arm, cracked some ribs and managed some head trauma. It could have been so much worse, so we have been thanking God ever since."

"I don't doubt that. And how are you doing? It's been so long since we've seen each other, I wish I could be there to help and comfort you."

"It's alright. There has just been so much going on lately with life, and work and the agent drop that I hadn't realized how much our relationship has been suffering."

"Whoa-whoa-whoa. What? Your agent dropped you? When did that happen? You didn't tell me that."

"Oh, yeah, I was going to tell you when we were going to go for supper, but I got a little side tracked with Dad's accident and all. They dropped me that morning."

Turner paused and took this new information in.

"I'm really sorry, Dixie," he said. "I hadn't realized you've been struggling that much with your writing. What are you going to do now?"

"I really don't know. I do know that I am going to take a bit of a break from it and let myself breathe. The stress has been too much lately. They haven't liked any of my work since my first book and I've been incredibly lost during the whole process of creating new stories. So, between that, and trying to keep enough shifts at the café, plus volunteering so much at the woman's shelter that I now realize that I haven't been putting in the effort to keep the bond between us strong. So, if you are up for it, I was thinking, maybe we could start having date night at least once or twice a week? It doesn't have to be anything fancy, just some time for us to spend together. I really do miss you."

"I think that's a great idea. The past few months have

been crazy with work on my end too and a weekly break to clear the head would be great. I miss you too, Dix. I'm glad that you are open to working on us. It means a lot. And I'm sorry that I've been so hard on you lately. If I had known how much you had been dealing with, I likely would have backed off. I'm sorry for that."

"Thank you. But Turner? I better go, I think I hear Mom and Dad pulling into the driveway. Thank you for understanding, and I miss you."

"I miss you, too. Call me when you get back? We will reschedule that date we missed."

"I'd like that. Bye."

"Bye."

I hung up the phone with a smile on my face and headed towards the open door where Demi stood, clearly excited.

"Hey, Daddy," Demi helped our mother bring him through the door and onto the couch before setting his crutches to the side of him.

"Thank you, you two. Now don't worry so much, I told you, Doreen, I will be fine. Sit and relax a bit."

"Don't tell me not to worry. It's my job to worry, as your wife. Now, do you need anything? A drink, some food? How is your pain? Do you need any medication?" she replied.

"Doreen," my father chuckled. "I'm *fine*. Why don't you go have a shower and relax a bit? You've been running around for days."

"Hmm," she responded before placing her purse on the counter and her jacket in the closet.

"How are you feeling, Dad?" I asked. "What exactly happened, anyway?"

"Yeah," Demi added. "I want to know, too."

Our dad, leaned back carefully into the couch and got comfortable. "Well," he said. "I was simply coming back from a business meeting in the city when the semi coming towards me, blew a front tire and began to swerve. Within seconds, the driver began to lose control and swerved into my side of the road and before I could react, we collided. I don't remember anything after that, other than waking on the way to the hospital in pain. The EMTs gave me some meds to ease the pain and as soon as I got to the hospital they sent me in for x-rays and all sorts of fun tests before fixing up my leg."

"That's so scary." Demi whispered.

"It was something, alright," he smiled. "But, nothing to worry about. Just have to thank the big guy upstairs that it wasn't my time to go quite yet."

"We've been praying and thanking God ever since Mom called," I told him. "I'm really happy that you are alright."

"Thanks, dear. Now, did you two find something to eat while you were here? I hope you helped yourselves."

"We did. Don't worry," Demi smiled and got off her chair. As she did so, the doorbell rang. "Who is that?" She gave a funny look and ran to answer the door.

Once the door was opened, to everyone's surprise, standing awkwardly and holding a bouquet of flowers, was Amber.

Everyone paused what they were doing and stared.

"Um, hi. I hope that this isn't a bad time," Amber said. "I heard about your dad and thought I should bring these over."

"Oh, yeah. Sure thing. Come in," Demi stammered, clearly confused.

"Thank you so much, Amber. What a thoughtful gesture," our mother walked towards Amber, giving her a hug.

Amber gave her the flowers and stood in the foyer, clearly uncomfortable. "How are you feeling Mr. Churn? You're looking alright."

"I'm feeling well, thank you, Amber. How are you doing these days? I haven't seen you in a long time."

"Oh, you know. I'm alright, busy working at the

restaurant and going to school."

"Oh? What are you going to school for?" Our mother asked while she put the flowers into a vase and set them on the counter.

"For business management," she replied. "I've decided that I'd like to open up my own restaurant once I'm finished." She gave a weak smile. "There are these girls I know that decided to chase their dreams, so after many months of thought. I decided to give it a try as well."

Both Demi and I stared at Amber, clearly speechless. Our father noticed what was going on and spoke up. "Doreen? Would you like to help me up to the bedroom? I think I could use a nap, and I'm sure you would like a shower after being in that hospital for the past few days."

Mom, picked up on that cue and helped our Dad to the bedroom while the three of us stood in the living room.

"I'm glad you are doing something good for yourself," I finally said after a silent minute.

"Thanks. Um, I just want to say something while I'm here with you guys." She paused and looked down, playing with her fingernails. "I'm really sorry about everything that happened between us." She then looked us in the face, tears forming in her eyes. "I never wanted any of this. I never wanted to hurt you and I never wanted us to not be friends. You two were my best friends growing up and it's been killing me that we don't talk anymore. I wish I could take back every mean thing I've said and I wish that none of this had ever happened."

"Oh, Amber," Demi walked over to embrace her. "It's okay."

"No, Demi," she held her tightly. "It's not okay. What Miranda and I did to you two was wrong. We were upset that you two were moving on in life and we said many mean things and," she sniffed. "I'm just really sorry."

My heart sank a little as I watched the tears stream down Amber's face. I walked over to hug her as well.

"It's alright," I said. "We forgive you."

"Yeah," Demi said. "The past is the past."

"Really?" Amber asked and wiped her face with her sleeve and smiled. "You guys. Since our fight, I have been completely miserable. The reason I sided with Miranda all this time was because, without you two, I had no one left in this town. I couldn't risk losing my only friend left. And honestly, the only way Miranda and I managed to last as long as we did, was because I did what she said. We got into it after you guys left after the funeral. I told her that what she was doing to you two was wrong and that I wasn't going to put up with it and let her treat you that way anymore. So, after that, she told me off and I decided to do like you two and chase my dreams. Which is why I packed up and went to Winnipeg to further my schooling. I figured if I did this, then maybe my own life would feel fulfilled. But, I knew that I couldn't ever fully move on without fixing our relationship."

Demi and myself stood there, speechless. "So, if you two aren't talking anymore, where is she?" I asked.

"Oh, she's still working at the restaurant in town. She found some new girls to hang out with and apparently, parties... *a lot* now. We haven't spoken since I decided to go to university."

"Oh." I said. "Well, it's good to hear that you are doing something for yourself. You deserve to be happy."

"Thanks. It feels really good to be on my own and doing what my heart leads me to do, rather than doing what someone else tells me to. I see why you two left now. I just want to say that I'm super proud of you and I hope that one day maybe we can be friends like we used to?"

"Absolutely." Demi smiled widely. "I think I would like that, don't you, Dix?"

"Totally. Maybe during spring break, you can come out to visit? You can stay with us and our roommate if you'd like." I offer in return.

"I think that would be wonderful. Thank you, guys."

We all embraced each other one more time. "Well, I better get running. I told my mom that I would help her with some yard work today. You two take care okay? And text me... I miss you two." She began to walk towards the door.

"We will. And Amber?" I asked.

"Yeah?" She paused with the door partly open.

"Thanks. For everything." I smiled.

"No, thank you." She then walked out the door and shut it gently behind her.

Demi and I stood there staring at each other, clearly impressed with what had just happened.

"Did not expect that one," Demi piped up first. "I'm glad that just happened but...wow."

"Yeah, I'm kind of speechless too, but at the same time very happy. Maybe this is a sign that things are about to start looking up for me. Well, and you, too."

"I know what you mean and I think it very well could be. Just have to keep our heads up and continue to look forward, right?"

"Right."

Later that evening, as my family and I sat around the fireplace in the living room, glasses of wine in hand, we finally got a chance to catch up on all that had been happening the past few months.

"Yeah, so now that I've been dropped by my agent, down to working two to three days a week, Turner and I are struggling, it's been quite the past while. But, I'm trying to keep my head up and believe that something better is on its way. It can't stay crappy for forever, right?"

"Oh, I'm sure things will start to look up before you know it," My mother offered. "Since they dropped you and you don't know where to look for another, have you ever thought about self-publishing? I've read on the internet that apparently its becoming a big thing these days. It might be worth considering."

"I've honestly never thought of that before… and I'm not sure why I haven't. I'll definitely consider it. Thanks, Mom."

"Or," my Dad interrupted. "Have you ever thought about starting your own company?"

"What do you mean?" I asked.

"Well, you say that there aren't many agents out there and finding a place to publish here in Canada, why don't you start your own company? Learn how to self-publish and what not, you can go to school for your English literature if you need and why not start your own publishing company? Might seem crazy, but worth a thought."

"Start my own company?" I asked "Are you crazy? How on earth would I do that?"

"I really don't know, hun, but it would be worth looking into, don't you think? Everyone starts from scratch at some point in their lives."

I thought about that for a minute. "That has to be the craziest thing I've ever had someone tell me…but I think I might just think on it…Thanks."

"And what about you, hun?" Mom asked Demi. "How have things been going for you?"

"Oh, you know, work has been slow. Well, the modeling has been anyway. Work at the store is great, I get to see all the new products before anyone else and the girls I work with are always enjoyable to be around too. I do wish I could find more gigs with my modeling though. There are a lot of rules and standards to reach before you even qualify for what most companies look for. It's tough in the modeling world, that's for sure. I don't know how Aunty Lisa did so well. She must have had a great agent behind her. I wish I could find one to help me out."

"I'm sorry that you two are having such difficulties with life right now. I remember when I was your age and just starting out in interior decorating. Getting my name out was one of the hardest things I had to do." Mom offered. "But, I just kept at it and after a few years I found my success. You two have to just keep fighting and try new approaches to what you are already after."

"Like what do you mean, Mom?" Demi asked.

"Like your Dad said, Dixie, if you consider starting your own company maybe, new doors will open for you. Who knows, maybe you could do the same one day. If you don't like the rules and how the modeling industry runs, what better way to fix it than to change it yourself? You know, your grandma always told me that if I don't like something, then I need to find a way to change it, myself. So, now I'm going to tell you two the same thing."

She paused and looked over at our Dad and they both smiled. "We know what you two are capable of. It is in your blood to do great things. Aunty Lisa is looking down on you two, guiding you and watching over to make sure you are taking the right path in life. We all want you to do great things and we don't want something as small as an agent drop to detour you from what you are meant to have in life. Do you understand?"

I thought about what she had just said and looked over at Demi, "Well, what do you think? Should we pull a crazy and change the way things are run?"

Demi took a deep breath and rubbed her head. "If anyone knows us and what we are capable of doing, its these two. Mom, Dad, if you think we can honestly pull something like both of those ideas off, I think the least we could do is give it a try. It never hurts to try, right?"

"That's my girl," Dad beamed. "And if you two ever need any help, financially, or any other way, don't be afraid to give us a call. We will be behind you every step of the way. Remember that, okay?"

I took a sip of my wine and smiled once again. "Thanks, Dad. You guys are the best."

"Well, it's been a long few days, I think I'm going to tuck in for the night. You girls can stay up and continue your hen party, but I'm off." Dad said as he slowly pulled himself off the couch and grabbed his crutches.

"Here, let me help you." Mom put her half empty glass of wine down and got up to help Dad to bed. "You girls can shut the lights off when you go to sleep right?"

"Of course. Feel better and love you two," I replied.

"Love you, too. Good night." They both slowly made their way to their bedroom at the end of the hallway and shut the door behind them.

"Well…We definitely have a lot to think about now, don't we?" Demi took another sip from her glass and curled up underneath her throw blanket.

"Yeah, do you really think we could pull something so big off? I don't have any idea where to even begin something like that, start our own companies, I mean."

"Well, maybe it's time that we practice what we preach. Maybe it's time to pull all our faith and believe that, like Mom said, Aunty is guiding us. God is guiding us and everything happens for a reason. You got dropped, I can't find enough gigs, Dad got hit by a truck and now suddenly both, Mom *and* Dad are pushing us to start our own businesses? You cannot tell me that it's just a *coincidence* because you and I both know that there is no such thing."

I ran my fingers through my hair, "You're right. Well, we will think long and hard on both options. Either continue and hope for the best with what we are doing or, like they said, change it ourselves. Neither road is going to be easy, Dem. I hope you know that."

"Obviously. But it'll be worth it." She then raised her glass. "Cheers to new beginnings."

Chapter Fifteen

Months had gone by and things had finally begun to look up. Both Demi and I had decided to go ahead with our parent's advice and start to change the way the modeling and publishing industries ran; well, to try, at least. Demi had picked up extra shifts at the boutique she worked in, so that she could afford a new camera and set up to start photographing models of her choice.

I, however, dove into researching everything I could about starting your own publishing company and I must say, I had more work cut out for me than I had thought. It would take me longer to get going because, to be honest, I wasn't one hundred percent sure on *how* the entire industry ran. I didn't understand why some work was chosen and some wasn't. So, I figured, to fully understand how the publishing industry worked and to make more connections, I needed to work within it. I quit my job at the café and found a publishing company downtown that would hire me as a junior editor, where I could work five days a week, nine to five, and would learn a lot in a very short amount of time even if the pay was terrible.

Hey, we all have to start somewhere, right? I thought that if I could understand *why* my writing was rejected, maybe I could help other people, including myself, get their work published. Not only that, but Turner and I had been steadily seeing each other two to three times a week, sometimes more and were working on 'us'. He had even come down to the shelter the odd time to volunteer with me.

Life had been finally starting to look up and I have to admit, I hadn't been happier than I was at that moment, in a very long time.

"So," I said, "I've been working on a business plan

lately and decided that when I get my own company up and running. I want to be able to donate to the woman's shelter when I have enough business."

"I think that would be cool," Turner replied as he, and I, Demi, Logan, and Naomi sat around our living room one evening, sipping homemade cocktails. "You do enjoy volunteering there."

"Yeah, and by the looks of it, they could use some funding."

"So, how is the business plan coming along, anyway?" Naomi piped up as she sat cross legged on the recliner, tucked in the corner of the sun-lit room.

"Slowly," I sighed. "I've been working steadily on it when I get some free time. I have to go to the bank to see if I can get a loan but I still need to save a little bit more and get a few more hours in at work before moving ahead. I don't want to have to ask Mom and Dad to help me unless I have to. But, everything else seems to be going fine. I already have a business name, and the plan is in the process. Once I get everything figured out, I will publish my own work and then get my name out to do other help other people achieve the same goal. Most days I feel I am in way over my head, but then I remember that everyone who's ever done anything big in life has likely felt this way. It makes me feel a little better anyway." I leaned back and rested my head on Turner's arm that was draped over my shoulders.

"Sounds like a challenge, but I'm sure you'll figure it out. Rome wasn't built in a day, right?" Logan commented, as he sat down on the couch, glass of water in hand. "Your sister is still figuring it all out too, aren't you?" He looked over at Demi to the left of him which also happened to be beside myself.

"Ugh, yeah," She said. "It's definitely something else. I have found a few women to model for me, only, my issue is that I can't pay my models very large sums. But thankfully, the girls I have found don't seem to mind. They understand that I'm starting out new and luckily, fully support me. Most women and men that I've talked to about starting my own agency think that it's cool that I am willing to photograph all body types. I'm not setting up many rules or standards that you *have* to meet to before I even think of capturing someone. I think it would boost a lot of people's self-esteem if they saw more women and men of all shapes, sizes, colors, whatever. You know? So, right now, I'm mostly working on building a massive portfolio and down the road, who knows, maybe my work will be featured in magazines and online for people to see around the world. That's the goal anyway."

"Well, I think that is an amazing goal, Dem." Naomi smiled. "Both of you are challenging such big industries, and it gives me goosebumps seeing how your hearts are into it. You both are going to do incredible things and it'll be enjoyable to look back on all this one day, knowing where you both are starting out. I'm really proud to be known as your friend," She beamed.

"You're sweet, Naomi. Thank you." I smiled.

"Yeah, thanks." Demi said. "But it is you guys that keep us going most days. It's hard and a lot of the time, well, I know this goes for me anyway, but it's knowing that you and our parents believe in us so much that keeps us going. Lots of days, I feel like I'm crazy to attempt such a task, but knowing you have my back, really helps. So, thank you, all, for that." She looked over to Logan. "And thank you for sticking with me even though I have such crazy dreams."

"I'm not going anywhere," He said. "I'm with you until we are old and wrinkly." He made a silly face, pulled Demi in closer and kissed her on the forehead.

"So, now that we know where you two are headed, how about we order some Chinese food?" Turner offered.

"I think that's a great plan. Does everyone want the usual?" I asked as I got up from the couch and wandered over to the kitchen where the phone sat on the counter.

* * *

The next day happened to be Saturday, so because I had the day off from editing, I decided to spend the first part of the day relaxing with coffee in hand on the living room couch, whilst reading the book *You are a Badass* by Jen Sincero as Demi was working and Naomi had gone for a walk. The second half of the day was spent with Turner at the Canadian National Exhibition also known as the CNE or the Ex.

I had never gone nor heard of it before so Turner told me that I was definitely up for an exciting treat. Upon arriving, my mind was blown away at the amount of activities there as well as the number of people that attended. The CNE is an eighteen day even that took place along Toronto's waterfront on the shores of Lake Ontario and just west of down town Toronto.

The day was hot and muggy being mid-August, but that didn't stop any of the attendees from enjoying themselves. Everywhere you looked, people were smiling and laughing while either enjoying one of the many snacks or simply touring around. As we entered the site, Turner grabbed hold of my hand and walked side by side with me throughout the crowds of people.

"So, what do you think?" Turner asked excitedly. "Have you ever seen anything like this before?"

"I haven't. Back home in Moville the largest event we have is the summer Fun Fair and we only get a couple hundred people stop by. There has to be thousands of people here," I smiled as I looked around. To the side of us, a group of kids were screaming and chasing each other with balloon swords while the parents sat at a picnic table enjoying some form of cold beverage. Ahead of us we saw carnival rides and heard some live entertainment blaring throughout the entire grounds. As I looked around some more, my heart began to fill with joy.

"I'm really glad you brought me here. This is the most

spectacular thing I've attended in a long time."

Turner squeezed my hand. "Well, just you wait. You haven't seen anything yet. This is simply the entrance. You haven't even seen half of this place yet. But, before we go any further, maybe we should grab a quick bite to eat and a couple bottles of water. The heat is insane and we are going to get thirsty later. Want to go check out those food trucks and see what they have to offer?"

With that, we headed over to a group of crowded food trucks where Turner ordered some pulled pork and I decided on a bacon cheeseburger. We sat and ate at a picnic table for twenty minutes before buying an extra water bottle each and heading off into what was to me, the unknown.

The rest of the afternoon flew by. I couldn't count the miles we had put in. We walked all the way down to the waterfront to watch some of the sports events that had taken place, then we wandered around the many exhibits and displays before checking out the shops and carnival rides.

After going on many rides, we found ourselves sitting atop the Ferris wheel, watching the sun go down. Turner had his arm wrapped around me and my head on his shoulder. The air was starting to chill for the night so we snuggled in close.

"So, now that you've officially experienced the Exhibition, what do you think now?" He asked.

"It's definitely something else," I replied. "I'm glad I got to see what it's all about. And I'm really glad that I had you to experience it with. So, thank you." I looked up at him and gazed into his gorgeous blue eyes.

"No, thank you, Dixie. These past few weeks that we have been spending more and more time together really means a lot. I've enjoyed hanging out with you." He smiled, staring back.

"Me too. It's pretty clear how much we were both

missing out on each other."

"Agreed. And it really got me thinking how much you mean to me," He began to play with a stray lock of my long hair. "Dixie…"

"Yes?" I asked. Suddenly becoming concerned at the look on his face. "What? What is it?"

He sat, silent, while still playing with my hair. "I, um…"

"Yes?" I asked again. Only this time, confused.

He looked up again, deep into my eyes and blurted out, "I love you."

I froze in place, unsure if I had heard him correctly, "What?" was all I could get past the shock.

"I love you, Dixie. More than anything in this world." He paused again. "I know we haven't been dating that long, but I've never had feelings like this for anybody else. When I'm away at home, or at work, all I can seem to think about is you and your smile and laugh. You make me feel…complete, as cliché as that is. I just wanted you to know that."

I then broke out into a smile and a tear of joy rolled down my cheek. "I love you, too, Turner."

It was then his turn to smile.

"I think of you the same way. Whenever I'm at home, or work, or volunteering, I always wish that you were beside me. I love our inside jokes, how you comfort me when I feel I'm going crazy, trying to start by own business, how you are there for everything. I don't want to be with anyone else. Ever."

Turner then gently put his hand on my neck, under my ear and slowly pulled me closer and kissed me more passionately than he ever had before. It felt as though time had stopped at even though there were thousands of people below us, it was like we were the only two people on the entire Exhibition grounds.

After leaving the CNE, we caught the TTC back to

my place. Demi texted me earlier saying that she was going to spend the night with Logan and Naomi left a note on the counter saying she wouldn't be home until late that night and not to stay up for her, and, knowing Naomi, that meant 2:00am or later. We had the place to ourselves so Turner and I decided to put on a movie cuddle up on the couch with a blanket and a bowl of popcorn.

"This is one of my favorite movies," I say part way into the movie. "It makes my heart flutter seeing how much Noah loves Ali. He would do anything for her if he knew it'd make her happy."

"Yeah, it's pretty good. And Ali loves him just as much. Kind of like me and you," Turner smiled down at me on the couch and scrunched his nose as I lay on his chest.

"Just like me and you," I say back. "Popcorn?" I offer a piece and feed it to him.

"Thanks. Dixie, can I ask you a question? When you see yourself down he road, five, ten years from now, what do you see?"

I thought about that for a moment. "Hmm," I said. "Well, I see myself in a gorgeous house somewhere here in Toronto with you. Maybe a child or two. I see my publishing company doing well, same with your landscaping, and over all, I see happiness. Why? What do you see?"

He stared at me again with his gorgeous blue eyes with the same look he gave me when we first met, that one that made my heart skip a beat every time he did it.

"I see the same thing," he paused. "I see you and me and some kids living the most incredible life imaginable. I know that starting business is and has been tough but can you promise me something, Dix?"

"Anything," I said.

"Can you promise me that even though you're about to get busy with your publishing company, that you will always make time for us? We were struggling before, and I don't ever want us to go through that again."

"I promise. As long as you promise to be understanding that some days I will get busy and will need time to catch up on whatever I'm working on. Your work is seasonal, whereas mine will go full bore year around. I need to know that you will understand that."

"I do. Thank you."

"Thank *you*, we are a team and we need to be there for each other and be understanding when times get chaotic. That's what makes a relationship stronger, right?"

"Right." He said, again with *that* look.

I smiled again, "What?" I asked.

"What?" he asked me back.

"You have that look in your eye. The same one you had when we first met. What are you thinking?"

He continued to stare at me for a few seconds before answering. "I'm just thinking of how lucky I am to be with someone as amazing as you. You're so intelligent, thoughtful, outgoing but yet laid back. You're just...perfect. For me, that is, and when I told you earlier that I loved you, I hope you know that I meant it. Truly and deeply from the bottom of my heart." He then held me tightly.

"I meant it, too, Turner. You mean the world to me and I don't want to spend my life with anyone else." My eyes began to sparkle in the dimly lit room.

Turner then grabbed by chin, lifted my face up and began to kiss me passionately. My heart began to flutter and I had a sense of calm rush over me. We kissed for a good minute or two before I pulled away and stared at him.

"What's wrong?" he asked, clearly confused.

"Come with me." I said.

"Where?"

I stood up from the couch and tossed the blanket to the side of the couch before blowing out the candles and turning off the T.V. I reached for his hand and pulled him gently off the couch.

He then realized what was going on and his eyes widened slightly, "Dix, are you sure? I mean, we don't have to if you're not- "

I cut him off. "I'm sure. Now shut up and come with me."

Turner followed, holding my hand, into the bedroom, where we shut the door and spent the rest of the night making love until we, finally, fell asleep in each other's arms.

Chapter Sixteen

"I can't believe today is actually here," I thought to myself as I laid awake in my bed staring at the daylight that was shining though my bedroom window. The room was filled with the sun's warmth as it sparkled on the frosted windows and reflected from the light grey painted walls that I had finally finished less than a week ago.

Before I moved here to Toronto six years ago, not knowing a single soul; not knowing exactly how I was even going to make it on my own. I had known nothing about the city, let alone how to get around. All I knew was that I would find a way. I felt it in my heart that some way, somehow, I would make it into his new world I was about to create, and to my surprise, I had done just that.

My phone suddenly began vibrating on my night stand beside me. It was Naomi, the text read: "RISE AND SHINE SLEEPING BEAUTY!!! TODAY'S THE BIG DAY! I'LL BE THERE IN TEN WITH COFFEE."

I rolled out of my comfy, king-sized bed and sat on the edge with my feet touching the white shag rug. Stretching and scratching my head tiredly, I brushed the hair out of my face and headed to the bathroom. I looked around and stare at the new shower, two-man bathtub and vanity before me. The white and grey marble that surrounds me is breathtaking. I loved the splashes of fuchsia in the flowers by the sink and in the towels by the shower; the color makes me happy. I smiled at all of my hard work that had clearly paid off, and walked to the sink to brush my teeth. From there I slip out of my pajamas and step into the shower to wake myself up.

Ten minutes later the front door slammed shut. "Lovey, I'm here! Are you up? You better be, I texted you fifteen minutes ago!"

"I'm in the shower! I'll be out in two," I yelled out.

I could hear Naomi moving around the kitchen before she walked down the hallway to my room.

"White Chocolate Mocha for you, peppermint tea for Demi, whenever she gets here and a Dark Cherry Mocha for myself. Noting but the best for us."

Naomi handed me my *grande* cappuccino as I stepped out of the bathroom wrapped in my towel. "Beautiful day out there. The sun is shining; the birds are chirping and there isn't one cloud in the sky. And it isn't even that cold out either for being the middle of December. Oh, and I talked to Demi, she said she should be here shortly. She was cleaning the house before Logan gets home from their guys' trip."

"Oh, good." I walked over to my dresser to grab some clothes. "And thank you by the way, for the coffee."

"Any time. So, are you excited to see Turner? They've been gone for what, a week now?"

"Yeah, a week too long. The house is so empty and quiet with him gone, Nai. Its honestly starting to drive me crazy. Like, okay, I'm not here *all* day long, because I'm at work most of the time, but the evenings really do get lonely. I wish he were home already."

Naomi took a sip of her coffee. "I don't doubt that. He will be here before you know it. You are a good woman, actually both you and Demi are, for letting them go away and have guy time in Vegas. A lot of women would struggle with the idea of their men leaving to such place, especially for what Vegas is known for."

"I know, but I trust him and he trusts me. I know he wouldn't do anything stupid. And if he did, I know that he would come home and tell me like he does every year."

Naomi smiled. "You two are adorable."

"Yeah…" I trailed off.

"What's wrong, Dix?" Naomi asked concerned.

My mind was so full; it took me a moment to realize I was staring blindly in my underwear drawer.

Grabbing the essentials, I tugged them on under my

bath towel and turned back to Naomi. "I need him, Nai. Is that weird?"

"Dix, he's going to be home tonight, you don't need to wor-"

"No, Nai. Not just like, need him home. I *need* him in the sense that I want to marry him. Is that weird? We've been together for five years now, bought a house together and he still hasn't asked me to marry him. Demi and Logan got engaged this spring and are planning a summer wedding for next year. I don't know, maybe I'm just envious. I'm the older sister and should be married first, isn't that how it goes?"

"Well, not always. I'm sure he will ask sooner or later, Dix. He probably is waiting for the perfect time. And seeing as your sister and Logan just got engaged this year, he probably doesn't want to steal their limelight. He likely wants them to enjoy their engaged time and not spoil it too soon for them by asking you the same thing. Do you know what I mean?"

I stared at her and thought about what she just said before squinting. "You know something, don't you?" I asked suspicious.

Naomi quickly looked away and took another sip of her coffee, "I know nothing."

"You're a liar. Naomi, I've known you as long as I've been in this city and if I know anything, it's when you are lying. Now, what do you know?" I crossed my arms and stared her down with a smirk on my face.

Naomi began to laugh. "I swear, I know nothing!" She then tried to change the subject. "Now, what are you wearing for your speech today?"

"Mm-hm. You're the biggest liar ever. But that's okay, I don't want to know anyway. I don't want to ruin whatever Turner might have planned. If he's planned anything." I turned and headed towards the fireplace in my room before turning it on and stepping into my walk-in closet. "But anyway, Turner is coming home today, just in time for my Christmas supper at work, and our theme is a black and white tie affair, so I want to look extra glam after my speech this afternoon."

"Oh, that reminds me," Naomi quickly hopped up from my bed and set her drink on my night stand. "I bought a couple new dresses the other day and brought them here for you to try on. Here, let me get them." With that, she scurried out of my room and down the hallway to the kitchen where she left her bags.

Within the minute, Naomi returned holding a bag that clearly contained a dress.

"What is that?" I asked, curious as usual.

Naomi smiled. "Here, I thought you might need something new to wear for your speech today." I began to unzip the bag, slowly. "If you have something already picked out, then you don't have to wear it…" She said as she sat back down on my bed, waiting to see the expression on my face once I got the bag fully open.

"Oh. My. Gosh! Is this…" my eyes widened and my mouth dropped as I pulled the dress out of the bag. The dress sparkled in the sunlight and left little rainbows all over my bedroom. It was a cocktail length, long sleeved, beige dress that had sparkling floral details all over it. "How did you? Naomi, this is the dress Brittany Spears wore to the People's Choice Awards back in 2014. How did you find this?"

"Well, when you are in the real estate business, much like myself, you meet a ton of interesting new people. A woman I sold a house for, is friends with the designer, Mikael D. She told me that she would be attending a fashion show of his a couple weeks ago and asked me to join her. So, because I had no idea who Mikael D was, I googled him and his work and found this dress in his gallery. I knew your speech was coming up and I knew you loved this dress because I might have creeped your vision board once or twice when you weren't looking, and saw it there. So, when I found out who the designer was that made it and attended his fashion show, I luckily got to introduce myself and then bought one afterward," she beamed.

I ran my fingers over the floral detailing and hugged the dress tightly. With tears in my eyes, I thanked Naomi. "You are the best friend I could ever have. Thank you so much, Nai. I... I can't believe this right now."

"So, like I said, you don't have to wear it-"

"Oh, no, I'm wearing it!" I exclaimed. "I'm wearing it to my speech and I'm wearing it to my Christmas supper tonight too. Heck I might wear this every day for the rest of my life. It's so beautiful."

"Well, I'm glad you like it."

"I love it, Nai. But you really didn't have to do this. It must have cost you a fortune."

"Look, Dixie. I would not be where I am today if it weren't for you. You're the reason my real estate business has sky rocketed. The reason I drive my BMW and the reason not only I, but all three of us girls, have our dream homes. If you hadn't helped me so much these past few years I would still be sitting in that old apartment building working as a bartender at that crappy, run down bar, getting nowhere fast in life. But because of you, I could make every dream I had become today's reality, including moving my mother into a nicer home of her own. Due to that, I do believe that this is the least I could do. Tonight is a special night and I know that you fell in love with that dress forever ago, so I pulled a few strings and got it for you. And I figured what a better time than to wear it tonight?"

My heart melted as she said all of this to me. I looked at the dress once again.

"Okay, but only because you insist." I smiled cheerfully. "Help me try it on?"

"Absolutely,"

She then jumped off the bed and took the bag from me before I handed her the dress. Again, another dream come true. I then slipped on the dress and Naomi zipped it up for me. Luckily, it fit like a glove.

"How does it look? I asked eagerly.

"Ridiculously perfect! I can't believe how amazing you look in it! Go look in the mirror!"

I excitedly hurried over to the mirror in my walk in closed and gave myself a look over. The dress not only looked and fit amazing, but it felt incredibly comfortable as well.

"It's perfect, Nai. Absolutely perfect. And you know what? I have the perfect pair of Jimmy Choo's to go with this. You don't think it will be too much, do you?"

"You know, it could be just a tad, but isn't that what your speech is about? Getting what you want in life and making your dreams come true?" Naomi grabbed her coffee off of the night stand and took a sip.

"Well, yeah," I bit my lip.

"Then why would you wear anything else? I know you've been wanting this dress for forever and I saw those shoes on your vision board a few years ago. So why wouldn't you wear what you've manifested? This will be the perfect example that you are trying to set." She did have a very good point. "Wear it. Not just for me, but wear it for your audience. You deserve it. And hey, if you wear it tonight, guaranteed Turner won't be able to keep his eyes off of you when he gets to your supper."

I couldn't help smiling.

"Okay, help me take this dress off for now then and when Demi gets here we can go grab some brunch before we head to the auditorium. I'm starving."

Naomi chuckled. "Deal." She placed her coffee down once again and got up to help me take the dress off where I put it back on its hanger and hung it on my bedroom door.

"Totally random, but I picked up a new book the other day. None of what we published, but it's by a woman named Carrie Green. Her book is called *She Means*

Business and it explains her way of starting a business. I really wish it had been out when I first started my company because it has so many great pointers, some of which I have been applying lately." I went into the closet to find something to wear to brunch.

"Oh? That does sound like an interesting read. Do you have it here, at home?"

"Yeah, bottom shelf, under my night stand," Naomi looked down below and pulled the book out to study it. "Since reading it, I've decided to add meeting her to my vision board. I feel as though her energy is kick ass and decided that I just have to meet her as crazy as that might sound. I feel like we would have a lot in common."

"This is why I love you," Naomi laughed.

"Why is that?" I asked as I slid into something appropriate.

"Because you never leave room for doubt. For the 'what ifs', or 'maybe' or 'if I'm lucky'. You decide it's going to happen and you don't stop until it appears in your life. Carrie might be your latest biggest inspiration, but, you my dear, you are mine. Speaking of manifesting. Did I mention to you what I plan to manifest next?"

I then walked out of my closet and into the bathroom to towel dry and brush my hair. "You mean to be the biggest and most well-known real estate agent in all of Toronto? You did mention it about a month ago over coffee."

"No, not that one. I've decided it's time to find my soul-mate."

I dropped everything. "Excuse me?" I walked out of the bathroom. "Really? Oh, my goodness, that's so exciting, Nai! What made you want to find him now? I thought you liked being your own independent woman and living life on your own."

I sat on the edge of my bed facing Naomi. I touched her hands with pure excitement on my face.

"Well, I've been thinking lately. My career is close to

where I want it. I have my dream vehicle, I have my dream home and job and I'm only twenty-nine. I figured that it's time for the next stage in my life. It's time to find my other half so that I can share all of what I have accomplished. I don't want to die alone. You know what I mean? I don't want to turn into a crazy cat lady. I don't even like cats," she paused. "It's just…time."

"I completely understand. And I guarantee that he is around here somewhere. Toronto is *how* big? Surely he is out there, only you haven't met him yet. Who knows? Maybe you'll meet him later today at my speech, or at the Christmas dinner." I smiled supportively.

Right then the front door opened and in walked Demi.

"Hey, ladies, I'm here. Sorry I'm late." Demi called out as she closed the door behind her, took off her shoes and made her way towards my room where we both sat on the bed. "So, how pumped are we for today?" She looked down at my night stand where she saw her name on the tea Naomi picked up for her. "Oh, is this mine? Thank you. Oh and Mom messaged me earlier and said that there should be here in plenty of time. They told me they would get a taxi meet us at the auditorium for your big speech."

"What?! They are coming?" I said excitedly with wide eyes. "I am even more excited *now*. Today can't get any better."

"I bet it can, somehow." Naomi smiled.

"So, what were you two talking about?" Demi asked as she sipped her tea.

We were just talking about manifesting our special someones. Like you and Logan and Turner and I. Naomi says she's ready to find hers. Isn't that exciting?"

"Awe, Nai, that is way exciting. Have you started your list yet?"

"List?" she asked, looking from Demi to myself, confused.

"You know, your list of traits and qualities you want

in your special someone?" Demi sipped her tea once again.

"I didn't know I needed one."

"Um, yeah, it's super helpful and important. Didn't Dixie tell you about Turner?"

"No? What did you do? What happened?" Naomi asked.

"Oh, right! Well, you know how we met, right? I've told you that a handful of times. So, at first, I had an instant attraction to him and wasn't too sure why. I knew he was gorgeous and had an incredible butt but after meeting him at the park and then running into him here and there here in Toronto and eventually getting together, I knew he was what I was looking for.

"You know, when I first decided it was time for me to find my Mr. Right, I was sixteen. I wrote down every characteristic, trait and quirk I wanted in a guy, right down to the hair and eye color, the level of humor and how kind hearted I wanted him to be. And, honestly, the more I got to know Turner over the years the more I see almost everything I listed. He's honest, genuine, outgoing and ridiculously hilarious. He has that dirty blonde hair and bright blue eyes and that jaw line! Seriously guys, I think it's safe to say he's the definition of a panty dropper." Naomi laughed at that one. "And I swear on my grandfather's grave, he is going to be my husband one day. He just has to hurry up and realize this, too."

"Don't worry, Dix, when the time is right, he will be, if that's what you want." Naomi paused briefly. "So I guess I need to write down what I'm looking for in a guy, huh? You don't realize how…demanding us girls can be when it comes to what we look for in our other halves though."

Naomi bit the inside of her cheek as she stared at the floor, deep in thought.

"But you have to be if you want something as specific and as important as your soul mate or other half. If you just say you want someone who loves you, you will eventually get that. The problem with that is that because you weren't specific, you may find someone who yes, loves you, but does he love you for you or does he love your looks or a special trait about you? And, when you grow old together, your looks might change, or you might lose a specific way you do something. What happens then?"

Naomi shrugged her shoulders.

"I'll, tell you what, then he falls out of love with you. I have seen it many times over and nothing is more painful than watching someone go through a nasty divorce because the love is lost. You need to ask for your other half, the person with whom you are meant to live the rest of your life with, enjoyably. So, yes, it seems ridiculous writing literally every little trait down now but trust me, it will be completely worth it in the end. And the day Turner and I get married is the day I will repeat all of this. Now, the important thing to remember when manifesting, well anything, and I can never stress this enough is to never ever…"

"Settle," Naomi quickly spouted. "I understand and trust me, I would never settle for less than what I truly want and know I deserve. I just didn't know that you had to be *that* specific. I'm going to do some serious thinking over the weekend."

"As long as it's up to your standard. I hate when I see people settle for less than what they deserve. I just don't understand it. But, I know you are stronger and more patient than that. That is why you are going to find him, and you're going to have your happily ever after. But promise me one thing?"

"Okay, what?" Naomi asked.

"I get to be maid of honor."

Naomi looked at me as she started to get up, "Well, duh, you and Demi are my two favorite ladies. Who else would I have?"

"Just double checking." I giggled. "Alright, so you're driving, yes?" I asked Demi.

"You got it. It should still be warm from the drive

over here," she replied as she led us all down the hallway to the front door.

I then grabbed my dress, heels and purse as we headed out to door for some brunch, before we had to make our way to the auditorium to get ready for my speech this afternoon.

Chapter Seventeen

"Dixie? Are you ready? You're on in ten." A voice whispered from around one of the curtains.

"Yes, Mike," I replied as I breathed in as deeply as I could and exhaled all that was inside of me. "I cannot believe that this is actually happening! I've been waiting for this for months, since being asked to speak in the first place. Guys, are you sure I can do this?"

"You'll be fine! Trust me," Naomi grabbed both of my shoulders and stared directly into my eyes. "Now, what is your name?"

"Uhm, Dixie Churn?" I stated as I looked back at her, clearly confused.

"I can't hear you."

"Dixie Churn," I said a little a bit louder, but not so loud so that the people on the other side of the curtains could hear me.

"Right! And what do you do?"

I smiled as I realized what she was doing. "I am an author, publisher and now, motivational speaker."

"Now, what do you write and publish about?"

"Stories that inspire others to follow their dreams and to never give up, no matter what."

"Exactly. You can do this."

"Dix, you've been waiting for this moment for months. We've all gone over your speech fifty times with you, you have a killer outfit on, your hair is amazing and, frankly, I do believe that I am going to steal your shoes after today," Demi piped up. "You have absolutely nothing to worry about. Now go, have fun and we will be standing in the back watching you with Mom and Dad. She just texted me, saying that they made it. They had a delayed flight but managed to get here just in time. They said they will come find you after you're all finished."

"Oh, my gosh are you serious?" I asked, excited that my parents managed to make it to my big day. "Okay, you go say hi for me and I'll be waiting for you all in the back once we are all done."

From there, Naomi and Demi both gave me a hug, turned around, hurrying down the stairs and out the door into the auditorium.

As they both headed through the door, in walked Turner. My eyes widened and I ran toward him where he embraced me with a warm hug and the most beautiful bouquet of red roses I've ever seen. "Turner! What are you doing here?" I whispered. "You weren't supposed to be home from your trip until tonight."

He then smiled his gorgeous, freshly shaved smile. "God, you look amazing!" he exclaimed. Turner always knew how to make me feel special. "You know I wouldn't miss this for the world. I told the guys I had to come home early for your speech, so as understanding as everyone was, I caught a flight home this morning so that I could be here in time. You've worked so hard these past years and especially past few months, I wouldn't miss any part of it."

I gave him a look that said, 'Thank you' as I sniffed the bouquet of roses.

"Now, I'm going to go sit in the back with the girls and Logan, because, well, he wanted to see your speech too, and then after you're done here, we will all head to your Christmas party together. Sound good?"

"Sounds perfect. Thank you. For everything, Turner, and especially for coming today. I love you."

"I love you, too." He then kissed me deeply, slowly. "Now go rock that stage, but here, I'll take the flowers for now and we can put them in water after," he then grabbed the flowers, smacked my butt and headed towards his seat.

I stood on the corner of the stage behind the big red curtain and turned on my head piece microphone. 'This is it.' I thought to myself. I looked around and everyone seemed so content. The introductory speaker on stage was wrapping up her speech and the co-producer of the show was getting ready to count me in. Oh, goodness, I'm so nervous I think I might pee myself. What if I mess up? What if I freeze? No! I have waited too long for this, I am going to rock it, just like Naomi, Demi and Turner said.

The audience of eight hundred and fifty were applauding and I took a quick glance in the mirror beside the stage as Mike counted me in.

Here goes nothing. I walked out to the center of the stage. It's warm. My face felt flushed but there was no turning back. As the light shone down onto me I gained a certain amount of confidence from what seemed like out of nowhere. I knew that at that moment, that Aunt Lisa was there with me. So, I smiled and walked up to the stool with my latest book on it. When I glanced up I could see Naomi, Demi, Logan and Turner sitting in the back by a closed door.

"Good afternoon, ladies and gentlemen!" I exclaimed. "I hope you are all doing as fantastic as I am today. To start, I would like to thank each and every one of you for coming out today. For me, standing here, speaking to over eight hundred of you, is incredibly humbling as well as heart-warming. I have worked incredibly hard to get to where I am today. And I would like to share some insight on how to get from where you are to where you want to be in life.

"Do any of you have a goal? A dream? A wish that you would love to come true? Something that you can feel all the way from your head down to your toes but don't believe that it will ever happen? You think 'oh, I'm not smart enough', or 'I don't have the right job' or 'it's not in my cards'? Well, that is what we are going to talk about today. Making those dreams become a reality. Yes, I know, you've heard it a hundred times that dreams do come true, *yadda yadda yadda*. But sometimes it seems like they only come true for certain people. The rich. The famous.

Disney princesses. Everyone but you. Am I right?

"By the end of today, you are going to know how to make your dreams your reality. And if you don't have a dream already, you will find one before you know it."

The room was completely quiet. They are actually listening! Listening to me! Dixie Churn of small town Moville, Manitoba. The girl certain people said for years couldn't amount to anything. Couldn't publish a book. Couldn't travel the world. Couldn't stand in from of more than twenty people she went to school with let alone inspire them with her words of wisdom. Handfuls of people thought I was crazy for having such big dreams, for wanting more out of life than to work at the retirement home or the bank in town like everyone else for the rest of my life.

"When I was a young girl, I grew up in a small town where no one believed that miracles could happen to regular people. Everyone had that small-town mentality where this is life, so get used to it. Nothing exciting ever happened to anyone unless you bought one of the small businesses on main street. That was when everyone was happy for you, but then they would talk behind your back about how good or bad a job you were doing. Does this sounds familiar to anyone? Yeah, not so exciting, is it?

"Even though this is what I grew up learning about life, I never truly believed it was true. I always had expensive taste and had a great imagination. Two things everyone thought was humorous. A lady in the town I grew up in used to joke with me and tell me to grab my canoe and start paddling overseas to marry Prince Harry because that's about the only way my biggest dreams would come true. I would then laugh because I knew that wasn't true. I didn't know how, but I always told myself that I am going to do something big. Something so big that everybody's mind would be blown. Including my own. And you know what? I did. I stand here today with three best-selling books as well as my own publishing company,

DC publishing. *Now* people ask me how to do it, how I did it and how they can do it, too."

Everyone started to applaud and I couldn't help but break out in what happened to be the biggest smile I've ever had. "Thank you. And you know what? I wouldn't change a thing for the world. I've learn how to create the life I want to live. The life that is perfect for me, and now I am going to teach each of you how to create your own perfect life."

I briefly paused and then moved forward where the lights weren't shining in my eyes. I pointed to a lady sitting right in the front. "You, ma'am. If you could have anything in the world, what would it be?" Just then, one of the people running the show, ran up and handed the lady a microphone of her own.

"Oh, um," she replied. "I would probably have my mortgage paid off. Um, a new car and for my business to pick up again."

"Is that all?" I asked.

"I think so."

The same man who gave her the microphone, took it back with a nod.

"Very good. And you, sir, you with the blue tie." The same man who took the microphone, now handed it to the next person. "What is your greatest wish?"

"Well, my greatest wish would be for my brother's health to get better, the love of my life to find me and a house on the beach."

"Thank you, and you, ma'am?" I now shift my gaze to a younger woman sitting also, in the front row. "What about you?" I smiled encouragingly.

She looked up at me with hope that shone brightly in her eyes. Confidently, she replied. "My biggest wish is to become a plastic surgeon. So that I can help accident victims reclaim their lives. But, in order to do that, I need money so I can go to school. And I need a car so that I can get there. I've already been accepted but have no way to get there or to pay for it."

I stare down at her from the stage with the light partially shining in my eyes, and my heart filled with warmth, "What if I told you that you will go to school and that you will be able to pay for it as well as find a car? And you sir, what if I told you that you *can* potentially help your brother? Your other half and that gorgeous house might just be around the corner. And ma'am, your mortgage? Paid. That new car? It's in your driveway. And your business? Has never been more successful." Everyone was listening and staring, only now, confused.

"Everything any of us could ever want is ours. All we have to do is ask the universe for it. ask God for it. Whichever Is more comfortable for you and believe within our hearts that it will appear. We must ask because, if we don't ask, how can we receive? This is what is best known as the law of attraction and manifestation, or as I would like to also call it, praying. I speak in prayer. However, if one is not comfortable with speaking of God for whatever reason, whether it be for religious reasons or that you are just not one to bring God into your world, you can always call on the universe. It's pretty well the same thing, only a different name in my books. Whichever term you use will work just as fine which all of you will understand if you have read my previous books.

"However, it's not just a simple 'Dear God, I would like a new house', or 'Oh mighty universe bring me that new barbeque I saw in last week's flyer'." A few people chuckled at that one. "No, you have to *feel* it within your soul. You must believe that whatever it is that you are asking for is already yours. If you want something badly enough you must be willing to stop at absolutely nothing to get it. If it's a better job that you are wanting, you aren't going to just sit around and hope a new, better job falls into your lap, will you? No, you are going to, first, ask for it and put it out into the universe that you want a new, better job. Be specific here. Whatever it is that you ask for and believe in, is what you will get.

"You all have wished upon a star at one point in your lives, right? Well, that is somewhat how the law of attraction works. Whenever you wish upon a star you simply see a shooting star, make a wish and then wait for it to come true. Only, as a child, you likely would have forgotten about your wish until it magically showed up one day. That is exactly how you manifest things today. You knew how to manifest back then and didn't realize it. Only now, your number of wishes is unlimited.

"However, make sure that you are asking in the correct manner. If you ask for a new job and you only say 'I want a new job,' then you might stumble upon a new one but after working for a few days or a week or a month, you realize that this wasn't the job you asked for. You didn't want one that you had to get up at five o'clock in the morning to be at. You didn't want one that gave you only a thirty thousand dollar a year wage. In a way, you did just ask for it. All you asked for was a new job, you weren't specific in the job that you wanted. Did you mean that you wanted a career with a three hundred thousand dollar a year salary? A career that you simply love and enjoy? Did you want a job that feels like a second home to you when you show up to work in the morning? If that is what you want, then you must *say* all of this.

"So, that is the first stage of the whole manifesting process. From there, you are going to feel as though you already have whatever it is that you've asked for. You are going to wake up every morning and do your regular routine only, now, it's going to be a lot more enjoyable because you are going to act as though you are getting ready for the new, fun, high paying career that you asked God or the universe for. But you aren't just going to simply *act* as though you are off to your new job. You need to make yourself *believe* that is where you are going. Are you excited? Are you happy? Are you bursting with joy? If that is what you would feel if it had already occurred, then that is what you need to feel now. So, as you get dressed in the morning and feel like smiling, like dancing, like jumping up and down, then do it!

"The final stage is that you are now ready to accept and receive what you've asked for. This is where patience comes into play and trust me, no one will have as tough of time accepting this as I did. It took me a lot of trial and error before I mastered patience. So, you have now *asked* the universe for your new, exciting, high-paying career which you absolutely love. You *feel* and *believe* that it is already yours and you've already accepted the position. All you have to do now is allow yourself to be open to new opportunities that come your way no matter how big or small they might seem. You cannot allow fear, jealousy, or any other negative emotion into your life that could distract you from your goal otherwise you won't be able to manifest what is it you want.

"Now, you all are probably wondering how long it takes to manifest something. I honestly cannot tell you or even speculate about how fast any of this could happen. It's more up to each of you and your soul's journey to determine that. If you feel it in your heart that your desires will occur within the day or month or year, then that is when it could potentially happen. You cannot leave room for doubt if your heart gives you an answer. If you leave even the slightest crack for doubt to seep in, then you are going to be waiting a while longer. You must have one hundred percent faith in whatever it is you are after. Have faith that it will happen, that it will appear. And believe it or not, it will.

"However, now I am going to confuse you a little bit by saying that just because you ask for something doesn't mean it *will* always happen and there can be various reasons for this. The first reason could be that you want it *too* much. You are putting far too much effort into making whatever it is you want, a reality. By doing this and trying excessively to create this dream, that it puts up an energetic block rather than allowing it to come into your life. Now, don't ask me how or why, but that's just how it works.

"The second reason you might not be able to manifest something is because it might not be on your own personal soul's journey. You see, before we all come down to Earth, God pre-plans our soul's journey. From the life, we have growing up, to when we discover something about ourselves, to when we gain and lose weight, to literally everything. So, if you happen to want something and it just doesn't appear ever after a very extended time, just note that there is a reason it's not showing up in your life and might just be because it might not be on your journey…"

Chapter Eighteen

Upon arriving to the Christmas party after my speech, the weather turned for the worse and a mild snow storm began to settle in for the night. We crawled out of our vehicles and scurried inside as I fiddled with the keys to our new office building in which I would run my publishing business.

Turner helped me out of my jacket as I stomped my feet on the mat in front of the door to knock the snow from my heels. The entire group of us hung our jackets on coat racks along the wall just within the doorway. Thankfully, everyone was already dressed up from my speech, so we didn't have to worry about changing after the rush to get to my office building.

"Dixie!" my mother exclaimed as she hung up her jacket. "Look at this place. It is absolutely stunning."

The interior of the building was breath taking. The white walls and pale hardwood flooring, accented with touches of gold and silver throughout the entire building was enough to grab anyone's attention. Once down the wide hallway, the space would open up and in the center of the opening, held a large, oak table that could seat at least ten people comfortably. This was where we would host meetings once a week to see where everyone was at on current projects. Off to the side, was a counter space which held a coffee machine, mugs, microwave and a small sink to wash our few dishes. A small fridge sat off to the side along with a water cooler. And at the head of the meeting room, sat a grand, electric marble fireplace. Surrounding the large room were smaller glass rooms so that every individual working for me could have their own private space to get as much work done as they could.

"Thanks, Mom. I learnt how to decorate from the best," I winked at her. "You don't think that after growing up with an interior decorator, I wouldn't pick up on a few things, did you?"

I placed the flowers that Turner bought me in a vase on the counter once we were fully inside.

"You did good, hun. And we couldn't be more proud of you," my Dad rubbed my shoulders as he stood behind me. "Now, would you like help with anything? We might as well make ourselves useful and help finish setting up if you need," he offered.

"Yeah, sure. I have a few more boxes of decorations in the back room to pull out and set up, plus make coffee, push the big table to the side and a few other small things."

Once I had the boxes of decorations out and everyone started on their small tasks, I turned on the fireplace, lit some candles, pulled out a few more chairs, helped push the meeting table off to the side and got a big pot of coffee going.

"Dixie?" Demi chimed. "Where would you like me to set up the photo booth?" She asked as she pulled out boxes of cameras, lights, tripods and a few props that she had dropped off the day before.

"How about in the corner by the fireplace?" I offered. "Would that work?"

Demi looked towards the front of the room, "Yeah, that should be perfect. Thanks. Logan, Naomi? Would you two like to help me set up?" she asked as she began to fill her arms with cameras and other pieces of equipment.

"Sure," Logan and Naomi said simultaneously and grabbed the rest of her boxes and supplies before heading to the corner.

Since Demi's own modeling agency has finally taken off, I figured it would be fun to have her photograph our evening and what better way than to capture people enjoying themselves, than through a photo booth? Demi, as helpful as she is, instantly agreed to help me out for the night. Plus, it could add more to her portfolio, which she couldn't turn down.

Roughly an hour into finishing up, the caterer and her crew showed up and instantly began to organize the food and snacks for our evening. They prepared appetizers in one of the smaller rooms and set up the food on the massive meeting table that we had pushed to the side.

Slowly, but surely, my team of employees began to arrive. One by one, they showed up and as they did so, I handed out glasses of champagne with my mom.

"You really outdid yourself, Dixie," one of my employees said to me as I handed out drinks and made sure everything else was perfect. Rebecca was one of my main editors. She was on the shorter side and only a few years older than me. She had perfect, long, brown hair that usually sported beachy waves. Her thick framed glasses sat upon her nose and her taste in fashion always left me envious. We had first met when I worked at my first editing job, she also disliked how the industry was operated, so once I told her my dreams of starting my own company, she instantly agreed to join my team when that day came.

"Oh, you know me, Rebecca. I strive for only the best," I smiled. "And this must be Robert?" I asked as a tall man in a black suit stood next to her with his arm around her waist.

"Indeed," Robert held out his hand and shook my own, firmly. "Pleasure to meet you, Dixie. I have heard a lot of good things about you."

"Now, that is something I like to hear," I cheerfully handed him a glass. "I've heard many wonderful things about you too, Robert. I'm so glad that you made it here tonight. Oh and Rebecca, this is my Mom, Doreen. And if you see a tall, older man walking around, that will be my Dad. And if he tells you some jokes, just go with it and laugh. He thinks he is funny," I winked.

My mother held out her hand to gently shake

Rebecca and Robert's hands. "Pleasure to meet you, Mrs. Churn," Rebecca replied.

"Oh, call me Doreen. Mrs. Churn makes me sound old," she chuckled.

"Pleasure to meet you, Doreen," Rebecca beamed.

"Congratulations on the wedding by the way," I offer to Robert. "Rebecca told me all about it. Mexico sounds like a lovely place to get married."

Robert looked down at his wife and smiled. "It was definitely something else, that's for sure. It was a busy day, but we wouldn't change it for the world."

"That's so great to hear. I'm happy for you two, and I can't wait to see pictures."

"Thanks, Dixie," Rebecca replied.

"Well, why don't you two go make yourself comfortable, snacks should be around shortly."

Rebecca nodded, held her drink with both hands and the couple then left to join the rest of the small crowd by the fireplace.

"They seem nice," my mom said softly as she smiled in the direction in which they just walked.

"They are. Well, why don't you take a glass of champagne yourself and go introduce yourself to a few more people. They are all very excited to meet you. I mentioned that you and Dad would be here for the party and everyone was interested in getting to know the two behind raising me."

"Oh, alright," Mom said. "Let me find your father first, I'm sure he is already introducing himself. I just hope he doesn't embarrass himself." She gave me a quick smirk and a nudge on the shoulder before she left to find my father in the crowd.

DC Publishing employed ten people plus myself, so by the time everyone brought themselves plus one, as well as my small group, the room was quite full. I walked around the room making sure everyone had something to drink and had made themselves comfortable.

"I think you should relax now," Turner said as he took the tray of drinks out of my hand and placed it on the counter, before handing me one.

"I'll get there. I just need to make sure everyone else is comfortable," I looked around the room and took in the warmth of the energy surrounding me. I beamed with pride knowing how far I have come with my business. From starting from scratch to hiring ten others to publishing handfuls of books in just a few years, blows my mind. Not only that but being able to not only call the people here my employees, but my friends, warms my heart. If it weren't for everyone here, my dreams wouldn't have become possible. I couldn't help but beam with gratitude.

"Everyone is fine, now come, mingle, have some fun. If anyone needs anything, they know where to find it," Turner then grabbed my hand and pulled me into the small crowd of people where we would mix, mingle, snack on appetisers and sip champagne for the next three hours.

Over all, the evening went by smoothly. The food was delicious, the company was wonderful, I got to meet a handful of my employee's significant others or friends which they had brought as dates. Plus, the photo booth was a big hit. Everyone had fun laughing, conversing and most importantly, relaxing after a busy year. As the evening began to creep up, I decided that it was time for a toast. I then asked Naomi to grab a box of cards from a separate room as I was about to make my toast.

I clinked my glass with a ring I was wearing as I stood at the head of the room. "I would just like everyone's attention please." The room slowly quieted. "First off, this toast is a little late, so I apologise for that. I would like to thank each and every one of you for coming out this evening. We have had a very busy year and I would like to say how proud I am of everyone who works here. We have hit a few milestones within the business and because of all of your hard work and dedication, we have made many authors dreams come true.

"DC Publishing wouldn't be what it is today if it weren't for all of you. You have not only helped our authors dreams come true but you also helped make my dreams a reality, and I cannot begin to express what that means to me. For years, I have dreamt of doing something big that would help and inspire others and, as of today, I can proudly look at where we are and all that we have accomplished and I can say that we did more than I ever imagined."

As I glanced around the room, I see the warm faces of everyone and realized then, exactly how much they all meant to me. Naomi stood by my side with a box of envelopes in hand.

"With that, I have a gift for each of you. As Naomi walks around, I'd like everyone who works here, to take an envelope." Naomi smiled and begun to walk around the room as people took envelopes one by one until the box was empty. "Now, to show you all just how much I appreciate you and what you do for me, I would like to gift each of you with a five-hundred-dollar bonus to celebrate our five years that we have been in business."

The small crowd gasped as they tore into their envelopes and Demi quickly begun to take pictures of everyone's reactions. "Are you serious?" One of the employees called out.

I beamed, knowing just how much they all appreciated the gift. "Again, thank you all for your hard work, now let's enjoy the rest of our evening!"

A round of applause echoed though out the building before everyone began to mingle once more. But just as the chatter started up, Turner piped up as he stood beside me.

"Um, sorry, there is one more announcement," he shouted as he raised both hands into the air to make sure he caught everyone's attention.

Everyone turned in confusion towards Turner, including myself.

"What's going on, Hun?" I asked quietly.

Turner then turned to look at me once the crowd silenced once more. He smiled with a twinkle in his eye. "As most of you all know, Dixie and I have been together for quite some time now. We had started dating shortly after she first moved to the city. That means, that I have seen her ups, I have seen her downs and everything in between. As long as I've known you Dixie, you have been one of the most hardworking, dedicated and determined people I know," he paused and I glanced over at Demi, Naomi, Logan and my parents standing off to the side, smirks and smiles engraved onto their faces. Demi kept her camera up. I looked back at Turner, who stood beside me almost nervous, I still didn't understand what was going on.

"We have been through a lot, Dixie. It's been a tough ride for both of us with each running different businesses, your volunteering as often as you do," Everyone in the room chuckled because even after all this time, I still managed to volunteer at the woman's shelter downtown on my days off. "Not to mention all of the other small bumps in the road that we have had along this journey." He then grabbed my glass, set it to the side on a table and looked me directly in the eyes. "Dixie…even after all of this time, I wouldn't want to have gone through any of that with anyone else. And I look ahead and all I ever see is you. Your smile, your laugh, the way you welcome me at the door whenever you beat me home after work. I don't ever want any of that to change. So, I have a question for you." He knelt down and reached into his suit jacket, beads of sweat forming along his hair line.

I gasped and covered my mouth with both hands and instantly started to tear up.

"Dixie Churn…would you do me the honour of

becoming my wife? So, that we can continue to live this incredible life of ours, together?"

I then let the tears roll down my cheeks as I nodded 'yes'. "Yes, Turner. Yes."

He stood up and embraced me as the room began to cheer and lights from Demi's camera flashed continuously to capture this very moment.

My heart beat faster than it ever had as my parents both ran over to Tuner and I to congratulate us both with warm hugs.

"Oh, welcome to the family, Turner," my mother cried as she hugged him tightly before she turned to myself, hugged me and then grabbed my hand to admire the stunning diamond ring on my left hand.

"You did a good job," my father smiled and shook his hand.

"Thank you, sir," Turner replied.

"You both knew, didn't you!" I wiped the tears from my face as I asked them both.

My parents looked at each other, then at Turner before back at me unable to break their smiles. "Well, I couldn't ask for your hand, if I didn't okay it with your parents now, could I?" Turner held me around my waist. "Thank you both."

It was then Naomi's turn to butt in and congratulate me with a hug as Logan high-fived Turner and started talking with him.

"I *knew* you knew something," I squealed.

"You can't prove a thing," she smirked as she grabbed my hand. "He sure did a good job though, didn't he?"

"He did. Thank you for not spoiling it. I prefer this kind of surprise over knowing ahead of time any day." I beamed and wiped away a tear.

"I figured you would," she then gave Turner a hug before standing back and visiting with my parents.

Finally, it was Demi's turn to congratulate us. She set

her camera down on the mantle of the fireplace to look at the ring herself. "Oh my gosh, Dixie! We get to wedding plan together! How much fun will this be?"

"Right? We should share ideas so that we don't end up copying the each other."

"Definitely. Wow, Mom and Dad are going to be busy this upcoming year, hey?" We both smiled at them as Demi linked arms with me.

"They sure are. But you know what? If our marriages turn out half as good as theirs did, I'm sure we will be just fine," she paused. "I'm really glad I get to share this with you, Dix… Not just your engagement, but this life. I don't think either of us would be here if it weren't for us sticking together all of these years. You know, Thelma really knew what she was talking about when she told us to stick together," she said as she looked around the room at chattering people.

I looked into Demi's eyes as my own began to water again.

"I can't believe you remember her saying that," I smiled. "But you're right. We are a pretty kick ass team if you ask me. I love you, Dem."

"I love you too. Cheers to us."

The rest of the evening was spent chatting with everyone at the party where we all laughed, and continued to grow closer together as more than just a working a team. We grew together as a family who would work together for many years to come, making what we had created ten times bigger than I could ever imagine.

I guess Aunty Lisa was right when she said that if you always believe in yourself, any path you choose in life, *is* possible. It might take a little longer than you hope for, but if you keep pushing and never lose sight of your goal, literally any dream can come true if you want it badly enough.

ABOUT THE AUTHOR

Leteisha Anne lives in rural Manitoba with her fiancé and two children. After learning about the law of attraction in her teens, she has spent many years learning how to apply the principals to create the life of her dreams. By spending time in nature and connecting with God as well as her spiritual side, she has only just begun to create the life she has always wished for.

Made in the US^

Middl^